Triple Caste G
Book Or

He Never Told Her

Joseph Jethro

JOSEPH JETHRO

First published in Great Britain in 2024

ISBN: 978-1-917452-15-1

josephjethro45@outlook.com

Chapter One
Clad in black! Watch your back!

The ruthless rain viciously battered the police cars, and the drumming sound echoed throughout the stuffy air, which was filled with anxiety and tension. The policemen cautiously surrounded Diamond House, the beams of their police lights penetrating through the thick darkness, illuminating the mighty skyscraper towering above them.

The head officers, their faces etched with tension, gripped their guns tightly. The noise of helicopters hovering overhead reverberated throughout the vast space, drowning out the distant hum of traffic from the hectic New York streets beyond. Each thud of rotor blades added to the nerve-racking atmosphere, amplifying the urgency of their mission.

Sergent Andrew Armstrong's voice cut through the chaos. He was filled with desperation as he bellowed, 'We need backup from the NYSA right now!' His knuckles were pale, and the gun's weight was stressing him out. He wiped his sweat-soaked eyebrow and clenched his teeth nervously.

'Holy...!' cried out Officer Steven as a motorbike with two men came flying out of the enormous glass windows of Diamond House, sending the glass scattering everywhere, adding to the already tense situation.

The motorbike hit the ground, skidding past the police cars. The two men on the bike fired their guns, piercing holes into steel and bodies, forcing the policemen and head officers to seek refuge behind vehicles and ambulances.

'Shoot the living daylights out of them, man!' shouted Benjamin, reloading his mag and shooting brutally at the two men.

The tension hung heavy in the stuffy and humid air as the motorbike suddenly stopped behind a tree. One of the men fixed a cold gaze on Benjamin, his finger trembling on the trigger. Seizing the opportunity, he fired.

The bullet sliced through the air, shattering a police car's window before striking Benjamin in the leg.

'Ben, are you all right?' gasped Steven, running up to him. Panic clawed at his throat; his heavy footsteps splashed through puddles as he rushed towards Benjamin.

Benjamin's response was an awful mix of pain and anger, 'No, damn it, do I look all right? Be careful, Steve,' he warned, 'The two...riders are well-armed and protected.' As he uttered those words, the world around him blurred, a cacophony of sirens, shouts, and distant footsteps.

The pain in his leg was unbearable, a searing reminder of the bullet's cruel trajectory. His heartbeat was racing, intensifying his agony as if the very rhythm of life conspired against him.

Ben clenched his teeth, sweat mingling with the rivulets of blood that streamed down his left hand that was pressing down on his wound. The wet road beneath him seemed to absorb his suffering, its unforgiving surface pressing against his trembling body.

'Call the ambulance right now!' shouted Steven, glancing back at the officers, whose eyes were on the motorbike that had abruptly sped off from behind the tree.

'Here,' Steven sighed, making Benjamin hide behind a police car and shielding him from the other dangers lurking in the dark and stressful night.

But the nightmare was far from over; three more slick black motorbikes sped up the main road, shooting at anyone in their way. A vicious and brutal police chase started, filling the air with an ear-splitting and deafening noise. The three motorbikes artfully spread out, taking different and confusing ways.

Rain continued to fall relentlessly, a curtain of silver threads blurring the world beyond. Sergeant Andrew's authoritative voice boomed through the downpour. 'Do we have to call him?' he shouted in frustration.

Officer Joseph, soaked to the bone, nodded grimly. 'Yeah, we've got no choice,' he replied, raindrops clinging to his uniform. 'We need backup.'

Sergeant Andrew pulled his walkie-talkie out from its holster, anger showing up on his pale face. 'We're going to have to retreat if you don't call him right now!' he barked at somebody through the walkie-talkie, vexed.

Meanwhile, Steven looked up the street worriedly. 'The ambulance should be here soon,' he said, biting his bottom lip and glancing down at Ben, who was gritting his teeth in agony and pain. And then, like a beacon of salvation, the ambulance arrived. Its wailing siren cut through the wind, and the paramedics leapt out, their movements precise and urgent. Their neon-yellow jackets glowed in the grey deluge as they sprinted towards Ben.

'You'll be all right!' one of the paramedics shouted, her voice muffled by the rain. She knelt beside him, gloved hands probing his wound. 'We've got you.'

Steven, his face filled with concern, grabbed Ben's hand as they lifted him onto the stretcher. Rain plastered his hair against his forehead, and he struggled to catch his breath.

'You're going to be okay,' Steven said, his voice trembling.

The ambulance doors swung open, revealing a sterile interior. Fluorescent lights flickered, casting eerie shadows on the metal surfaces. Benjamin was carefully placed inside, and the paramedics followed, their movements coordinated. The doors slammed shut, muffling the rain and the chaos outside.

As the ambulance pulled away, its tyres hissing on the wet road, Steven stood there, rain streaming down his face. He wiped the sweat from his forehead with the back of his hand, a blend of relief and exhaustion washing over him. But then, something caught his attention. An SUV hurtled down the main road, its headlights slicing through the rain. It was going fast, reckless and dangerous. He squinted against the downpour, then sprinted towards Sergeant Andrew. 'There he is, Boss,' he panted, pointing a trembling finger at the speeding vehicle.

The slick black SUV with dark-tinted windows pulled up beside Sergeant Andrew. The window rolled down, revealing a young driver dressed in black.

A mischievous smirk decorated his face as he spoke, 'What's up, bro? I see you've run into a problem.'

'What are you smirking at, you stupid idiot? Don't waste time; get chasing those devilish bikers before everyone in New York gets killed!' shouted Andrew, his face turning red as a blazing fire.

The young man, dripping with confidence and audacity, burst into laughter, 'Got that bro! Ring me later if you've got my number!'

Arrogantly, he spat out of the window, put on his shades, and sped off, leaving everyone standing and staring at his SUV in bewilderment.

'I bloody hate that guy. Got the nerves to call me 'bro'!' yelled Andrew, sweating profusely.

Steven, ever the provocateur, teased, 'I think he's a cool dude,' he grinned, trying his best to provoke Andrew.

'Shut your gob. We've got to get to the head office before it gets blown up!' Andrew shouted cheekily, jumping into his Range Rover and driving off.

Meanwhile, Officer Joseph, who was standing next to Steven, suddenly received an urgent update from Officer Kate, who was standing nearby: 'Officer Joseph, the young man's on the chase. I've been informed,' she announced, clutching her motorbike helmet. 'We've bugged his car to keep an eye on what he's doing.'

'Good,' said Joseph, 'And yeah, Kate, keep up with your crazy work. That was such a good move you made saving those kids that nearly got killed by those evil men who were on the motorbikes,' he sighed with relief.

Kate swung her leg over her sleek motorbike, the engine purring to life. She secured her helmet, the visor reflecting her determined eyes. 'Thanks, Officer,' she said, her voice steady. 'I'll carry on trying my best,' she added, 'Please tell my brother, Benjamin, that I'll be visiting him after work.' Her voice wavered, revealing the depth of her worry.

Joseph looked at her sorrowfully and said, 'When I visit him in the hospital, I'll pass him your message,' he promised. 'Pray that I don't get killed.' Fear gnawed at him, but he pushed it aside.

Chapter Two
He's got the gun! You gotta run!

'I think they've lost us, Loukas,' Ned exclaimed mockingly, his hands tightly gripping the motorbike handlebars as he sped up the motorway. 'Those jerks don't stand a chance against us.'

'It was good that we chose motorbikes for our mission. Otherwise, stealing all these expensive diamonds from Diamond House would have been difficult. And yeah, don't forget about the most valuable ruby in the world,' Loukas laughed, holding onto Ned's shoulders.

Ned suddenly accelerated, breaking the speed limit and whizzing in and out of lanes like some crazy drunk, causing inconvenience for all the motorway users.

'I got my foot blasted! It bloody kills!' groaned Loukas, looking down at his destroyed shoe. One of the officers had shot him, and the bullet had ripped through his shoe and flesh.

Loukas leaned down, touching it gently. Instantly, blood stained his hand. His wound was deep, and it stung like crazy as the wind blew against it.

'Well, lucky for me, I didn't get shot! Stupid cops couldn't even aim properly,' Ned boasted with triumph.

'You sure got away with it!' came a sudden contemptuous voice, booming straight towards them.

'What the...? You're so close to our motorbike!' shouted Ned frenziedly as his eyes caught sight of an SUV driving close to their motorbike.

'Oh! I sure am.' Before they could even react, the young man driving the SUV rolled his window fully down, and in one swift motion, he aimed his gun and fired an unforgiving bullet straight at the motorbike's back tyre.

The impact of the bullet sent the motorbike skidding into the motorway barrier; its screeching tyres filled the air with an uneasy noise.

With a quick hand, the young man veered his big vehicle towards the fallen motorbike, which was lying on its side, with the two men sprawled on the floor in a terrible state.

The young man slammed his foot on the brakes, causing the SUV to skid to a stop. He proudly swung his door open and arrogantly flicked his black hair back as he leapt out of his SUV. 'Yo, dudes. Do you want a cuppa or a couple of punches?' he laughed, walking towards the two men as he pulled his gun out from his thigh holster.

Ned, who was sprawled on the cold, damp floor, with blood trickling from his head and nose, tried to reach for his gun, which had slid an arm's length away from him. His fingers twitched, their movements feeble and desperate.

The young man, clad in black, sneered down at Ned. His laughter echoed through the cold night, striking fear in his heart. 'Oh! No, you don't! I think you've forgotten who I am,' he exclaimed, stepping on Ned's hand to prevent him from reaching his gun.

Ned's anger flared, 'Triple Caste Gangster!' he shouted, lifting his head slightly, 'I laugh in your face!'

The young man's eyes narrowed, 'And I laugh in the face of evil,' he leered, lifting his gun and aiming it at Ned's head, ready to shoot.

'No, you don't, TCG!' shouted Loukas, who had silently crept from behind. With one sudden movement, he grabbed Tipple Caste Gangster by the neck and attempted to strangle him, 'You're always interfering, TCG. You're a piece of hell.'

'You want to know what hell is? Let me take you six feet down; then you'll sure find out what hell is.' TCG suddenly spun around, violently striking Loukas directly on his face with the butt of his gun, sending him crashing on the wet floor. He shot Loukas in the head and turned around to shoot Ned, but to his amazement, Ned was surprisingly standing behind him and, with one sudden movement, sent his huge fist crashing straight into TCG's nose. Instantly, blood gushed out, dripping unpleasantly on the floor.

'Oh, so you wanna play dirty? I'll show you how to play, you ass wipe!' he shouted, holding his gun tightly; he grabbed Ned's head and slammed the gun straight into his nose. Seeing his nose bleed didn't satisfy him at all; he grabbed Ned by his hair and smashed his face onto his knee, aggressively repeating it multiple times. Blood poured, bones broke, and then, with one swift movement, he threw him on the floor, shooting him dead.

'Two idiots down, three more idiots to go,' muttered TCG. He knelt and started rummaging in Ned's pockets, pulling out a pocketknife, a cig box and his phone. 'I think the head office will need this as evidence,' he sighed, shoving the phone into his pocket. He quickly ran towards his SUV and jumped inside.

After driving for a while, TCG parked on a run-down street. He had been following two motorbikes for about five minutes, being careful so they did not suspect anything. He continued to observe them as they jumped off their motorbikes and walked off, disappearing into the thick darkness of the night.

TCG quietly jumped out of his SUV, both his hands clenching a gun. He stealthily crept into a narrow alley; suddenly, his sharp eyes caught sight of a spiral staircase ascending to a building's roof. Checking left and right, he continued walking into the dark alley.

He inhaled the cool breeze and quickly tip-toed up the metal stairs, trying his best not to make a sound. He was just about to step onto the roof when he heard two people whispering on the roof amongst themselves. He stood quietly and listened intensely.

'Did you tell Kevin where to hide the box of diamonds before we ship it to Mexico?'

'Sure, Dall. It's just about Kevin reaching the harbour before that bloody TCG catches up to him...'

'Don't worry about me catching up to him. First, think about what I'm going to do to you bastards,' shouted TCG from behind. He started shooting at the two men standing in the dark. They dived for cover, shooting back without any hesitation.

TCG swiftly ducked behind a water tank that stood on the roof. Bullets whizzed past him, and the two men started challenging him to come out from behind the tank, provoking him with horrible, nasty swears, but he did not fall for their trap.

The rooftop became a battleground, and TCG's heart pounded with adrenaline. The water tank provided scant cover, but it was better than nothing. He could hear the men closing in, their heavy footsteps thundering on the roof.

His fingers tightened around the grip of his gun. He had to be quick and decisive.

The first man stepped into view, eyes wide with determination; TCG pulled the trigger, and the gunshot reverberated, striking the man in the head, causing him to crumple to the ground, blood staining the rooftop.

But there was no time to celebrate. The second man came running at him, moving like a soldier, gun raised, his eyes showing hatred. TCG knew he had to act fast; he aimed carefully and fired.

The bullet struck the man's leg, and he fell on his hands, screaming in pain.

TCG sprinted, closing the distance between them, his adrenaline surging. The wounded man struggled to raise his gun but wasn't able to do so. TCG got his chance and fired again, hitting the man straight in the chest. The man's eyes went blank as he slumped to the ground with blood pouring out of his wound.

'Four idiots down, one more to go,' he whispered. Suddenly, his earpiece started beeping. He answered calmly, 'What's up?'

'We've been tracking you down, and you've done a great job. There is just the last guy left. He's the one who has the diamonds and the ruby,' came Joseph's voice.

'You don't need to worry. I've got him under wraps,' laughed TCG, sprinting down the metal stairs and legging it to his SUV.

'Oh yeah! Look up,' said Joseph.

TCG looked up as he sat in his vehicle and saw a helicopter flying above him. 'Sir Lustrum is watching you from his helicopter. That's how we've been tracking every move you make,' laughed Joseph. 'He is saying that you move as fast as a cheetah.'

TCG stepped on the gas and started speeding up a main road.

'Got to say, you've got some bad boy moves,' stated Joseph admiringly.

TCG didn't respond to Joseph's admiration. Instead, he pridefully remarked, 'I've got to go. I need to catch up to that asshole,' he smirked, glaring at a motorbike through his windscreen.

'Sure, be careful,' advised Joseph.

'Shut up, you don't need to worry about me!' TCG said. He put the call down and started following the motorbike.

After a while, TCG casually approached the motorbike. He calculated his move and then, with a sudden surge of determination, rammed the heavy vehicle into the motorbike's rear wheel. The impact was explosive.

The motorbike skidded, twisted and buckled. Its rider catapulted into the air and landed on the pavement with a thud.

The motorbike continued skidding across the road, leaving a trail of sparks. It eventually collided with a lamppost, filling the air with a terrifying noise.

Meanwhile, the man managed to scramble towards a nearby bus stop, his hands scraping against the rough ground, causing them to bleed.

TCG parked over; he jumped out of the SUV, loudly swearing. 'Today, you pissheads have made me do some bad boy exercise,' he said sarcastically, 'Don't take me wrong; I really needed it. And there's one sweet word that I can't wait to hear. I think you should know what it is!' he laughed, walking up to the injured man.

He crouched down next to the man, grabbed his neck with one hand, and slammed his head against the bus stop pole.

TCG raised his gun, and with a smirk spreading across his face, he spoke, 'Why don't you tell me what the sweet word is? Then I promise I won't ever touch you again.' The man started to shake, gazing into TCG's jet-black eyes. 'Come on, man, who can resist a promise like that?'

The man's eyes widened as TCG's grip tightened around his neck. With panic, he started to stutter, 'The sweet word...is revenge...you always want revenge.'

'Yep, that's correct, and as I promised, I'm not going to touch you,' smiled TCG. The man felt relieved after he heard the words of reconciliation.

'But I'm going to bang the living daylights out of you! My middle name's brutal, ya ass wipe,' laughed TCG.

The man's eyes widened with fear. TCG put his finger on the trigger and shot the man in the head, silencing him forever.

Chapter Three
Clock ticks! Get the chick!

'Outstanding work, TCG. You should join our crew,' Officer Joseph laughed, clearly impressed by TCG's skills.

'You know me; I love sticking to the shadows, 'cause if I work with you shitheads, I'm going to end up sussing out your damn flaws, and if that happens, I'm going to have to shoot you in the head,' TCG smirked, putting his shades on and displaying his classic gangster attitude.

'Yep, that's the cool dude!' exclaimed Steven, looking at TCG admiringly as he jumped into his SUV and slammed the door shut.

TCG stuck his arm out the window and laughed mischievously, making everyone shiver. 'Oh yes, before I leave, Andrew bro, I want to give you some advice: focus on your enemy when you're trying to shoot, not on your toes.' Before Sergeant Andrew could respond, he revved his SUV and drove off with a sense of arrogance.

Andrew's face turned red as he blurted out, 'That cheeky idiot!'

'He doesn't care who he talks to,' Kate said, folding her arms.

'That guy's ego is off the charts!' yelled Andrew, sweat trickling down from his head.

'At least he got back the ruby and the diamonds for us,' said Joseph, trying to hide his smile.

'Yes, I agree, he did a good job,' sighed Andrew, his voice changing dramatically as he ran his fingers through his grey hair.

TCG relaxed on his bed, mindlessly flicking through his phone. The clock's rhythmic ticking echoed through the empty room, emphasising the passing of time.

He lifted his head and looked at the clock. Its needle pointed to nearly half past five in the evening. With a heavy sigh, he lazily got up from his bed and walked towards the distant corner of the room, where his desk stood.

He slowly opened one of the desk's compartments, revealing an array of deadly instruments neatly lined up in all sizes and shapes. They awaited his touch, their slick triggers promising power and danger.

His fingers brushed against the slick triggers, the icy touch of metal seeping into his very soul; in that lingering moment, he grabbed a compact, lethal handgun, concealing it within the depths of his cargo pants pocket.

With haste, he snatched his keys from the desk's surface. Unfortunately, his hand brushed against an award frame which was precariously perched on the desk. It fell on the glossy marble floor, shattering into delicate diamond-like fragments.

TCG sighed in frustration and leaned down to pick up the certificate. As he did so, his gaze fell upon another piece of paper amongst the shattered glass. Confusion seeped into his mind as he looked at the paper. Carefully picking it up, he realised it was a photo he had hidden behind the certificate a long time ago.

Time seemed to stand still as he stared at the picture, his eyes tracing the contours of happiness that now felt painfully distant.

Anger started flowing through his veins, overpowering the tenderness that once resided within him. In despair and fury, he tore the photo into four jagged pieces. With trembling hands, he crammed the torn fragments into the drawer, their destruction mirroring the shattered pieces of his heart.

He slammed the drawer shut, sealing away the remnants of happiness that were no longer in his heart.

'Past rubbish,' he muttered, striding down the stairs and into the hallway. He stepped into his trainers, zipped up his hoodie, and left the house.

TCG sat in his black SUV and drove smoothly out of the driveway. His earpiece started beeping, interrupting his bad mood; he answered the call with a heavy sigh, 'What's up? Officer Joseph!'

'I've received a message from one of the officers that something suspicious is happening near George Square.'

'How did he find out that there's something fishy going on?' asked TCG.

'The officer said that two men were sitting in a black Merc, and it seems like they were drug dealing,' replied Joseph, urgency in his voice.

'Sure, leave it on me,' TCG said, stepping on the gas and speeding through the traffic like a madman. People horned and swore at him, but he didn't care. He skipped through red lights, and it seemed like he was going to nearly hit a group of pedestrians crossing the road; fortunately for them, he had every move timed.

TCG quietly parked next to George Square; everything was silent, not a sign of danger. He could see a small family playing on the grass, dog walkers strolling with their dogs, and, as usual, cars driving in and out of the car park that was surrounded by loads of shops. TCG's eyes caught sight of some teenage lads hanging around in a gang. A particular teenager was acting big and hard and trying to amuse the rest of the gang. TCG recognised all their faces and looked around for any unusual activity.

He pressed the button on his earpiece and stated, 'Officer Joseph, are you there?'

'Any suspicious activity?' asked Joseph.

'There's nothing suspicious or anyone who can cause harm, and where the hell is that flippin' Merc that the officer had reported about?'

'Don't tell me it's driven off!' shouted Joseph in a pressing voice.

'Well, that's bloody shit. Why did that daft officer not keep an eye on the Merc? Is he mashed up?' shouted TCG.

'That guy never does his job right; he's probably gone to eat a doughnut from the local café,' suggested Joseph.

'Yeah, the fat shit,' sighed TCG. 'Anyway, I'll keep checking; it might still be here somewhere,' he stated, lowering his window.

A sudden feeling of curiosity ran through his veins. His gaze swept across his surroundings until it landed on an enigmatic sight: a young girl, totally new to him, sitting on a bench.

He watched as she absentmindedly twirled her blonde locks and hurriedly flicked through her phone. And then, unexpectedly, her eyes abruptly locked with TCG's penetrating stare.

It felt as though she knew he was scanning around for unusual activity.

Their electrifying connection lingered until TCG swiftly sealed off the outside world by rolling his tinted windows up, causing the girl to divert her gaze.

A shiver raced down his spine as he whispered beneath his breath, 'That was utterly bizarre.'

'What's up? Did you find any clue?'

TCG grabbed his head in surprise, 'I didn't know you were still on the call.'

'Don't worry about me. Have you found anything yet?' Joseph demanded.

'No...' Then unexpectedly, TCG saw it all: a man clad in a fashionable navy top and wearing a cap was dashing across George Square; his determination was evident in each powerful stride as he got closer to another individual whose intentions seemed uncertain as he sprinted towards the vulnerable girl sitting on the nearby bench.

Like a lightning strike, the man in the cap deftly dipped his hand into his pocket, withdrawing a sleek and gleaming firearm. In the blink of an eye, he fired, and a deafening shot rang out; the bullet skimmed past the other man, missing him by inches.

Despite the tension, the man who nearly got shot remained calm, swiftly revealing his gun; he quickly looked over his right shoulder for a few seconds, his determined gaze locked onto his pursuer, intensifying the enmity between them.

The young girl stared at them in astonishment, frightened by the noise of the firing.

As the two men got closer to her, a black Merc suddenly parked near the pavement where she was sitting.

The driver jumped out and shot the man wearing a cap straight in the chest, causing him to fall to his knees with unbearable pain running through his body.

The girl shrieked and attempted to escape, but the man who was being chased grabbed hold of her arm with a swift movement. He then pulled her head back and twisted her arms aggressively, causing her to let out another deafening shriek.

TCG emerged from his SUV like a dark shadow, his gun gleaming, ready to kill anyone who came in his way; the driver spun in panic and fired at TCG.

But TCG was a shadow, ducking with lethal grace; he did a flying kick straight in the driver's stomach and shot a bullet in his neck; the driver fell to the ground and remained there, bleeding to death.

The man holding the girl's arms pointed his gun at TCG and spoke harshly, 'I'm afraid you can't shoot me, ya bastard, because if you do, you'll end up shooting this!' He yanked the girl's head up, making her look towards TCG. Tears rolled down her face, and she quietly stared at him with worried eyes.

TCG lowered his gun and shouted, 'Let the girl go and take me instead!'

The man smirked, 'You think it's that easy?' His voice was a cold blade slicing through the air. He aimed his gun towards TCG and fired. A bullet sliced through the air, skimming his leg. He instantly fell backwards, screaming with severe pain.

The girl's captivating gaze bore into him as he fought to regain his footing. Consumed by rage, TCG unexpectedly swung his gun like a hammer, smashing it into the man's nose. The impact sent the man stumbling backwards, blood dripping from his nose.

But TCG wasn't done; two bullets found their mark, tearing through the man's shoulder; he released the girl and collapsed to the ground; she staggered to her feet and stared at TCG wide-eyed, fear decorating her features.

TCG couldn't help but stare at her as if a magnetic force had taken hold of his gaze.

Time seemed to stand still as his eyes focused on her, oblivious to the bustling activity around him. The girl's sheer presence had captivated him, leaving him in a state of curiosity and wonder.

His surroundings seemed to blur into the background as he tried to turn his face away from her. Then suddenly, TCG's gaze shifted towards five more figures emerging from the shadows; they were quickly closing in. His expression shifted from surprise to sheer disbelief. 'Leg it!' he urgently commanded.

The girl ran with all her might; her heart thumped hard against her ribcage, and her legs were full of energy. Her mind only focused on following the guy who had just saved her.

The world swirled into a blur behind them. There was a desperate race against time. TCG's breathing came in ragged bursts. Each step was like a battle against the odds and the encroaching darkness.

They ran side by side, the girl's determination mirroring TCG's unwavering resolve.

The sound of an army running behind them echoed in their ears, but they didn't look back; they couldn't afford to. Ahead of them lay uncertainty and danger, and the chance of survival looked grim. If only they could outrun the demons snapping at their heels.

'Get in the bloody car!' shouted TCG. She quickly yanked the back door of the SUV and jumped inside.

TCG jumped into the driver's seat, gasping for air. He started the car, quickly turned the steering wheel, and sped off. The girl shrieked and ducked her head as bullets ricocheted all over the windows.

'Don't worry, it's bulletproof,' TCG said calmly.

Chapter Four
Blossom, stop talkin'! You gotta get walkin'!

'What's happening? What's your status? Are you all right?' Officer Joseph's voice came through TCG's earpiece.

'I'll tell you later,' sighed TCG.

Joseph's frustration boiled over, 'What do you mean, tell me later? This is a mission; you're supposed to tell me what just happened back there!' he said, raising his voice for the first time.

'I know, bro! I don't want to talk about it now; I've run into a big problem, so just flipping listen to me before I bloody come after you, do you understand me?' shouted TCG, revving his SUV.

'Sure, Triple Caste Gangster,' Joseph retorted, then abruptly hung up.

There was silence in the air as TCG manoeuvred through the jam-packed New York streets, dodging cars and clumsy pedestrians.

'You all right back there?' asked TCG, glancing over his shoulder.

The girl's anger flared. 'Did you just say all right? Do you think I'll be all right after what happened back there?'

'Yes, obviously, that wasn't much of a biggie,' sighed TCG, looking down at his wounded leg.

'Are you taking the mick?' shouted the girl, flicking her hair back, 'And anyway, where are you taking me?' she asked, lowering her voice as TCG parked over, waiting for his automatic driveway gates to open.

'You don't need to know that.'

'What?'

'Shut your mouth before I shut it for you!' snapped TCG. The girl's eyes widened, her lips clamping shut as if TCG's words had the power to close them physically. The tension in the air was palpable, and she felt the weight of his authority.

TCG parked his SUV smoothly in his big driveway, the tyres smoothly rolling on the perfect asphalt.

Dipping below the horizon, the sun cast long shadows across the manicured lawn that flanked the driveway. The trees stood tall and imposing, their leaves rustling in the gentle breeze.

As the engine purred to a halt, TCG hopped out of the car with the grace of a man accustomed to luxury. 'Jump out, lass,' he instructed, opening her door. The girl stayed rooted in her spot and refused to move.

'Are you a baby? Don't you understand? Come on, walk!'

'I'm not moving!' replied the girl stubbornly.

TCG pulled his gun out, 'Ya need some encouragement!' She didn't say anything further and quietly followed his instructions. Silently, she trailed behind him. His arrogance grated on her nerves, the way he assumed she'd comply with his every whim. As he approached the imposing front door, she watched him extract a key from his pocket, the metal glinting in the sunlight. The lock yielded to his touch, and the door swung open, revealing a world of luxury beyond.

He glanced back at her, eyes assessing. 'You gonna move, or what?' he drawled, his tone dripping with condescension.

Her smirk widened. 'Inside? You really think I'm going in there willingly?' She locked eyes with him, challenging his authority. But before she could react, he seized her arm, his grip firm and unyielding. With a forceful tug, he pulled her across the threshold.

'Follow me,' he ordered, shutting the door behind them. The grand hallway stretched before them, polished marble underfoot and a crystal chandelier suspended overhead. She couldn't help but gawk at the richness and luxuriousness that enveloped her.

He swung the living room door open, and she stepped inside, her breathing quickening. 'So, is this your house?' Her voice dripped with sarcasm. 'You eccentric dude.' She swept her gaze around, taking in the plush furnishings, the art lining the walls, and the view of the manicured gardens beyond. 'It's massive! What are you, some crazy millionaire?' Her laughter was both mocking and genuine.

'You've got an attitude problem, haven't you?' sighed TCG, pulling his gun out and flinging it across the dining table.

'If you want to talk about attitude problems,' the girl's eyes flashed with anger. 'It's you that has an attitude problem. Didn't your mum teach you any manners?'

TCG slammed the glass of water he was holding on the dining table and shouted, 'Don't talk about me and my family. You don't know me!' He looked away from her and cautiously adjusted the window blinds, peering outside, 'We can't stay here for long,' he said, sighing heavily.

'What do you mean? I'm not going anywhere with you!' mocked the girl, taking a few steps back and leaning against the wall behind her.

'Why are you here?' asked TCG, walking towards the sofa.

'What do you mean, why am I here? You're the one who brought me here!' yelled the girl as she gave him a dirty look.

'No, I don't mean it like that; what I'm trying to say is, why have you moved to New York?'

'How do you know that I've recently moved to New York? New York is massive!' said the girl, eying him suspiciously.

'Shut up and answer my question!' yelled TCG, getting impatient with her.

'I came to study at a college,' she replied bluntly.

'Wait, what? How old are you?' TCG was taken aback. He had assumed she was much younger, perhaps a high school student.

'I'm eighteen. How old are you?'

'Thirty-five,' he replied, his eyes shining like sharp daggers ready to strike someone in the heart.

'Gosh, you don't talk much, do you?' she quipped, trying to break the tension.

She looked at him and smiled. Her smile was like a sunbeam breaking through storm clouds. It started at the corners of her lips, a gentle curve transforming her face. Her eyes sparkled, and the warmth in her expression reached deep into TCG's chest. It was the kind of smile that made time slow down.

His heart skipped a beat. He had never seen anyone smile like that before. It was as if she held a secret, a promise of something more. His breath caught in his throat; he was left speechless. The tension that had gripped him moments ago dissolved, replaced by a sense of wonder. He couldn't help but smile back, a mirror image of her radiance.

'My name's Liana,' she said, introducing herself. 'I'm British, and I live in London...' she hesitated and then questioned, 'What's your name?'

TCG looked directly at her; he weighed her words, assessing her like a predator seizing prey. 'Forget my real name; just call me TCG,' he stated bluntly.

'OK, Gangster!' Liana scoffed, rolling her eyes, but beneath her pride, fear gnawed at her insides. TCG wasn't just any guy; he was entirely something else.

The phone's ring tone shattered the silence, and his expression tightened. TCG answered calmly, 'What's up? Andrew, bro.'

'Triple Caste Gangster, I just belled you to see if you're doing fine,' said Andrew in his usual croaky voice.

'Sure, I'm chilling; it's just that I've been thinking if I should take a ferry or a plane,' sighed TCG, leaning his body against the sofa's arm.

'Just let me know when you've made your mind up. We'll get something done. And that bloody guy that you killed at George Square was dripping with blood, man! It was a mission cleaning him up,' laughed Andrew in a loud, disturbing voice.

'That's what happens when I blast them up,' laughed back TCG, his eyes flickering like the shadows dancing on the wall. He smiled wearily, and his lips formed into an unsettling grin.

'Anyway, Triple Caste Gangster,' Andrew continued, 'I need to get back to work. Call me when you need me.' The line went dead, leaving TCG sinking into a deep thought.

Liana took a few steps closer to the sofa, her curiosity overpowering her fear, 'Why in the world do they call you Triple Caste Gangster?'

'That's not for a little girl like you to know!' chuckled TCG.

'Wait, let me get this right, who are you?' sighed Liana frustratedly.

'Sorry, Princess, can't tell you that either,' TCG replied, his eyes flickering with memories of blood-soaked alleys and whispered oaths.

'Are you some type of three-faced gangster?' said Liana, perching on the sofa's arm beside TCG, her defiance masking her vulnerability.

'Sorry, Blossom. That is not for a little girl to know at all,' he replied, his gaze piercing her soul.

'Stop calling me a little girl! Do you understand me?' she yelled.

TCG rolled the bottom of his black cargo pants and winced as he glanced down at his shin; a jagged wound marred the skin. The pain radiated outward, sharp and insistent as if tiny needles were pricking at his nerves. The edges of the wound were inflamed, a fiery red that contrasted starkly with the colour of his skin. Each throb seemed to pulse through the gash, a reminder of the injury's presence.

The sensation was painful; the damaged tissue seemed to send distress signals to his brain. It wasn't a dull ache; it was harrowing, and his nerves screamed in protest. TCG's fingers trembled as he gingerly dabbed the wound; the touch was met with a surge of pain, like an electric shock shooting up his leg; he winced, gritting his teeth against the intensity.

The pain wasn't just physical; it gnawed at his resolve, chipping away at his mental strength, 'Ow, that's a killer!' he groaned.

Liana's voice, usually full of fear and urgency, now softened into a tender melody, 'Why did you risk your life by trying to rescue me?' she murmured, looking at TCG, her eyes searching his face for answers. They were a shade of cerulean that held the secrets of distant skies, their depths like the ocean's vastness, and they were full of peace and tranquillity. In their azure depths, one could lose themselves, finding solace in the tranquillity of her gaze.

Time seemed to stop at that moment, and the world's chaos faded into the background. TCG's heartbeat seemed to repeat her question, each thud a reminder of sacrifice and devotion. He met her gaze, and the weight of her vulnerability settled between them.

Like honey stirred into a cup of tea, her voice held a sweetness that removed pain and danger; it was the taste of trust.

Liana rested her hand on his shoulder. Her touch was both soothing and annoying, igniting a fire within him. 'And what were those men going to do? Like, what could I possibly have that they want from me?'

'Don't worry, pretty girl. That's my job, I like to protect people,' TCG said, rising. He moved towards a cluttered desk and swung open one of the compartments. He picked up a clean cloth and a bottle of antiseptic spray, his hands steady despite the turmoil inside him.

TCG winced as he dabbed the cloth against the wound, the sting sharp and immediate. Liana watched him, her eyes filled with concern. 'How's the pain?' she asked softly.

TCG shook his head and smirked. 'It's better,' he replied, though the pain was evident in his voice. 'But your constant questions are a real pain.' He sprayed the antiseptic onto the wound, the cool liquid hissing as it contacted his skin. The pain flared briefly, then subsided, leaving a dull ache. He then wrapped a bandage around his leg, his movements methodical and precise. After TCG finished bandaging his leg, he glanced at the desk, his eyes locking onto the handgun lying there. He picked it up and slid it into his thigh holster with a swift, practised motion. He straightened up, his posture exuding confidence and a hint of menace.

As he slowly approached Liana, his movements were calculated and fluid, each step radiating the confidence and swagger of a seasoned gangster. His eyes never left hers, a smirk playing on his lips. When he reached her, he leaned in close, his breath warm against her ear.

'Now zip it, and let's get going!' he whispered, his voice low and threatening. Each word dripped with authority and a touch of danger. The way he stared into her eyes sent a shiver down her spine, a mix of fear and excitement.

'Where are we going?' asked Liana, standing up.

TCG's eyes lingered on her, and he grinned. 'Just follow me,' he said, his voice filled with a hint of eagerness. He led her through the hallway and into a large room.

He did a hard walk towards the fireplace, where a frame rested. The frame contained a picture of a boy posing with his shades on; TCG grabbed it and started tapping his fingers on its surface as if dialling a number on his phone, his movements commanding and mysterious.

'What are you doing?' questioned Liana, putting her hand in front of the frame and blocking TCG's view.

'Move your hand, man!' he shouted, suddenly pushing her hand away, sending shivers down her spine.

'Wow, is that an iPhone disguised as a frame?' she gasped admiringly.

His voice was sly as he replied, 'I don't think you want to be standing there.'

Liana raised an eyebrow, daring him to explain further. 'Why not? Mr Picky!' she laughed, waving her finger at him. Suddenly, the floor beneath her shifted, causing her to lose balance. Panic gripped her as she flapped her arms wildly, desperately trying her best to regain her balance; she let out a startled shriek.

'I think you should've listened to me! What do you think?' laughed TCG, swiftly grabbing her hand.

'I don't care what you say, just pull me up!' yelled Liana, with a mix of frustration and fear.

His grip tightened, and he pulled her up with a smirk spreading across his face.

Her heart started beating faster as she gazed at the unexpected sight of stairs materialising from the floor, 'How did stairs just appear from the floor? Is that what you were fiddling about with that so-called frame?' she questioned, eyes locked on the marble steps leading downwards.

His voice cut through the air, 'No talking and let's get going,' he insisted, his tone filled with eagerness. TCG dashed down the stairs without wasting a second, leaving Liana staring at him with a frustrated face.

'Are you waiting for the stairs to disappear?' shouted TCG, his voice echoing with playfulness and impatience.

Liana sighed heavily and tip-toed quietly down the stairs, entering a vast underground tunnel.

The noise of their footsteps against the metal panels of the tunnel provided a strange metallic soundtrack, while the gentle hum of the blue LED lights above added a delicate ambience.

'What the...? This place is cool!' said Liana excitedly, listening to her voice echoing.

TCG pressed a button on his watch as they approached a garage, filling the air with a mechanical whirring sound.

As the garage door began to open, Liana couldn't believe her eyes; right in front of her was a hidden world of mechanical marvels and LED lights, illuminating the sleek curves and polished surfaces of cars.

Liana started breathing heavily as she stepped forward, her gaze sweeping across the row of glistening automotive artistry. She let out an enthusiastic comment that pierced through the air, 'Now those are some awesome cars, aren't they?' she laughed, causing TCG to playfully cover his ears before joining in with the laughter.

'Man, you talk loudly, don't you?' TCG grinned, 'I think I'll take the Lamborghini,' he said. He unexpectedly walked over to a slick metal box adorned with bright red LED lights.

He pressed his thumb against a small screen, and after a while, a synthesised robotic voice confirmed the correctness of his thumbprint. With a satisfying click, the lid of the metal box opened, revealing a concealed car key, 'Come on, jump in. We can't waste time,' smiled TCG, quickly grabbing the key.

Liana felt eager to sit inside the vehicle; the urgency in his voice made her feel like she was going on an adventure. She made herself comfortable in the passenger seat, and TCG softly shut the door, sealing her destiny for the thrilling ride that awaited her.

Chapter Five
The sea's not merry! Got a secret on the ferry!

'Where the hell are we going?' Liana shouted.

'Shut up, you little pest!' sighed TCG, his tone laced with frustration; he placed his hands on his head, fed up with her attitude.

'I'm not little, and I'm definitely not a pest,' said Liana, folding her arms.

'I'm gonna give you a ride home,' he answered, his voice calm.

Liana's eyes widened, pupils dilating like the moon's reflection in a still pond. The sound of home brought back tender and fractured memories. 'What do you mean by giving me a ride home?' she cried out, her voice trembling, the words hung heavy in the air, a plea wrapped in a blanket of fear.

TCG leaned back in his seat with one hand on the steering wheel. His lips curved into a half-smile, and she could see the cool dude image written all over his face, 'You'll be safe there, lass,' he said, his tone both comforting and caring.

Liana's confusion deepened as tears rolled down, 'I'm safe here, too,' she said, wiping away her tears as her fingers gripped the edge of the seat, 'What could I possibly have done that those men were trying to harm me?'

TCG's laughter cut through the tension; his gaze met hers, mocking and cold, 'Why don't you want to go home?' he taunted, each word a slap against her vulnerable heart.

As the car raced down the motorway, the world outside transformed into a blur, mirroring the whirlwind of emotions within Liana's shattered soul. Tears escaped her eyes, tracing vulnerable paths down her cheeks as she struggled with the overwhelming weight of her circumstances. There was a moment of silence; Liana continued to cry silently, and then she suddenly whispered, 'I don't have a home.'

'You sound like me,' giggled TCG, 'The only difference is, I'm not a big baby like you.'

'I'm not a baby,' replied Liana, her voice sounding adorable as she tucked her blonde hair behind her ear.

'Oh yes, you are,' beamed TCG, unable to contain his laughter.

He parked in a parking bay and whispered, 'We're here.'

Liana looked out of the Lamborghini window, 'It looks like you've just parked opposite a five-star hotel!' she said.

'You dope, that's exactly what I have done. Now come on, jump out, but don't forget to put your hoodie on,' he said, giving her a stern look. Surprisingly, Liana instantly obeyed without any further arguing.

As TCG and Liana walked towards the hotel, they were greeted by an impressive facade. The entrance was grand, with polished glass doors that automatically slid open as they approached it. The lobby was spacious, adorned with marble floors, elegant chandeliers, and plush seating. The air smelled faintly of fresh flowers from the arrangements on the reception desk.

At the reception, a friendly concierge welcomed them. The concierge wore a crisp uniform and stood behind a sleek counter. TCG handed over his identification, and Liana fidgeted with her phone, eager to explore. The concierge efficiently typed on the keyboard, confirming their reservation. He then handed TCG a key card, which had soft blue patterns engraved in it.

TCG and Liana walked towards the elevators. Pressing a button, the doors slid open, and they entered the glass elevator. Its walls were transparent, revealing a breathtaking view of the city. As they ascended, the lobby lights faded, replaced by the glittering skyline. Liana clung to the railing, her reflection merging with the city lights. TCG leaned against the glass, feeling weightless as they rose.

Exiting the elevator, they walked along plush carpeted corridors. The walls were adorned with abstract art, each telling a silent story. Liana ran her fingers along the textured wallpaper, marvelling at the delicate details. The soft lighting cast warm shadows, creating an intimate atmosphere.

They reached room 507. The door was solid wood, engraved with delicate patterns. TCG slid the key card into the slot, and the door clicked open. The room revealed itself, a sanctuary of comfort. They stepped inside, their eyes darting around the breath-taking room. TCG walked towards a plush sofa and sat down, stretching out his legs. Liana chose the opposite sofa, sinking into the soft cushions.

'My feet are killing me, man! I drove for bloody three long hours!' TCG complained, putting his tired feet up on the glass table.

Liana stared at him in disbelief but chose not to comment. Instead, she asked, 'So how long are we staying here for?'

'Officer Joseph is setting up something important that I need, which probably wouldn't take more than a few hours, so I suppose we will stay here for only a day.'

'So, you got any family?' Liana's question raised the tension in the room; she stared at him and waited for an answer.

TCG quietly stared at her as if he wanted to somehow make her vanish; his jet-black eyes looked towards the ceiling, and he flung his hands behind his head. His lips slowly moved, 'No, I'm a loaner.'

Liana pressed further, her curiosity building, 'Wait, what about your parents?'

'Don't talk about my family! Do you understand me?' shouted TCG, suddenly sitting up.

'Okay, dude! Calm down, what's the big deal? I just find you a bit strange,' she said, lowering her voice from the sudden bad-tempered response she had just received.

TCG's heart skipped a beat as he saw her face change dramatically; he knew he sounded harsh. 'How about you and your family?' he asked, trying to divert the attention off him. Nervously, he ran his fingers through his hair and stole side glances in her direction.

'Well...em, my mum died when I was a year old; I don't really remember her,' explained Liana.

'You seem like you're not upset about your mum,' he sighed.

'I do feel it, but I'm used to everyone around me saying she's dead, so I've just grown up in that state; you can't blame me, can you?' sighed Liana, fidgeting with her fingers.

'I see,' said TCG as he listened to her talk.

'I started living with my aunty, but when I was eleven, she died suffering from cancer, so I moved in with my grandma, who unfortunately is those typical granny witches that I flippin' hate,' said Liana, smiling mischievously, 'She's such a pain in the ass, the old hag.'

'What about your dad, you didn't mention him?'

'Don't even mention him...I hate him with all my heart!' Liana said with an attitude, quickly wiping away a tear. Her tearful eyes darted away from him, hoping he wouldn't notice her vulnerability.

'How can you say that about your dad?' TCG's voice was laced with condescension. He remained seated, taking a casual sip of Coke as if her anguish meant nothing to him.

'He abandoned me, and he never came to see how I was when I was going through so much pain and suffering, and then my aunt died, leaving me vulnerable and helpless. I would always cry that one day he would come and take me away from all this misery and sorrow, but the asshole never came,' cried Liana, sobbing her heart out.

TCG suddenly unleashed a fiery burst of laughter, a sound that echoed throughout the room. The intensity of his amusement caused him to nearly choke on his Coke; his loud laughter boomed with a mixture of amusement and disbelief as if he had stumbled upon the greatest joke in the world, 'Girls are such sissies!' he laughed, slapping his knee.

'Shut up, you jerk, you've never gone through what I've felt!' she yelled.

'I've gone through much worse pain than you, so take a chill pill,' smirked TCG, 'Now get some rest; tomorrow's going to be a big day,' he sighed, giving her a fake smile.

Liana stood on top of the ferry's deck and stared at the beautiful scenery. She inhaled the cool air infused with the scent of refreshing seawater.

Her blonde hair danced in the steady breeze, teasingly caressing her face. She was in a deep thought, lost in her own world. She suddenly returned to reality when she heard soft footsteps approaching from behind; she spun around and realised it was TCG.

'Hey, TCG. I've never been on a ferry before. It's so lovely,' she laughed, looking back at the sea, 'TCG, you're so lucky that you can just say, 'I'm going on a ferry, or I want to drive a sports car', and with a click of a finger, you get what you want.' Liana smiled, suddenly noticing a subtle change in TCG's expression, 'What are you thinking about?' she asked softly.

TCG hesitated, his gaze locked onto Liana's. 'I'm...well, I'm thinking about your smile,' he finally confessed.

'Why?' Liana said with curiosity.

He shrugged, 'I don't know... it makes me want to smile too.' His eyes softened as he turned and leaned on the ferry railing.

But as Liana continued to look into TCG's eyes, she realised that there was a magnetic intensity, a certain longing that seemed to appear from his gaze. Sensing a change, Liana couldn't help but modify her tone. Her voice was filled with deep curiosity. 'What's wrong? You seem worried,' she asked, her words dripping with concern.

TCG's focus remained fixed on Liana's electric blue eyes, momentarily lost in their depths; his voice dropped to a hushed whisper, 'I don't know...I don't think you should be out here,' he confessed, his grip on the ferry's railing started to tighten.

Caught off guard by TCG's sudden protectiveness, Liana's heart started to beat quicker, 'Shall I go in?' she asked, her voice filled with a hint of fear.

'Yes, but stick behind me and... and just keep your eyes open,' he urged.

Liana's heart thumped hard against her chest as she followed TCG through dimly lit corridors. Unease hung in the air, and her eyes darted nervously, searching for any sign of danger.

In the distance, she spotted the captain and his companion whispering secretly. Curiosity overwhelmed her, but little did she know the danger awaiting her. As if sensing her presence, the captain's piercing green eyes locked onto Liana's figure. Panic ran through her veins, freezing her brain.

His voice cut through the silence, causing her to shiver. 'Can I help you in any way, miss?'

'N-no,' she said nervously.

'You seem nervous, girl. Who are you with?'

'I'm with T... I'm with my mum,' she quickly said, pretending to follow a woman who was happily holding the hands of her two children.

'She's one funny girl, ain't she?' muttered the captain's companion, lifting his thick black eyebrow in thought.

Liana's fear intensified, and her heartbeat increased as she ran inside the room she was meant to be in, but the quiet room, which was once a haven of warmth and vibrancy, now felt cold and miserable.

Her fear intensified, and tendrils of panic wrapped around her like the mist outside; the polished wooden floor, once trodden by lively footsteps, felt cold and unforgiving under her trembling feet.

The air hung heavy, suffused with the scent of saltwater and lost hopes. The portholes, once framing picturesque views of the moon-kissed waves, now revealed only darkness, an abyss that mirrored her inner turmoil.

The silence was unnerving. Unable to bear it any longer, she cried out, her voice trembling with fear and longing: 'TCG!' Yet the room remained silent. She hoped he would hear her plea, but all she heard was her own voice, lost in the vastness of emptiness.

Liana's heart raced as a cold hand suddenly struck her in the face and then quickly covered her mouth, silencing her. She looked up and saw TCG staring at her in anger. 'Shut up!' he hissed.

Liana started panicking, fear and dread gripping her heart. She had trusted TCG and relied on him during this unforgiving journey, but now, his behaviour was erratic, and fear continued to gnaw at her insides, 'What's wrong with you?'

'Just shut up,' he repeated, pushing her out of his way. He barged towards the room door and double-checked to see if it was locked. 'Here, take this,' he said, shoving a cold, metallic object in her trembling hand, a weapon she had never held before, causing panic to rush through her veins.

'Are you out of your mind? Why are you giving me this?' she whispered.

'You're going to bloody need it,' his voice was low and urgent, 'Keep your eye on the enemy, hold your breath, then shoot. You'll succeed in your goal.'

Liana couldn't understand what was going on. The enemy? Who were they? And why was TCG acting like they were closing in on them?

'You're acting as if your enemy is already standing behind you,' she muttered, her fingers trembling around the gun's grip.

But before TCG could respond, an announcement echoed through the ship's speakers, cutting through the tension: 'All passengers, please come to the deck. Your captain would like to speak to you and show you the beautiful view of the vast ocean, a one-and-only lifetime experience.'

Liana felt her heartbeat quicken as TCG's grip tightened around her hand. The urgency in his voice sent shivers down her spine. 'Liana, has the captain seen you?' he asked in a panicked tone.

'Yes,' she replied, her voice barely audible, 'Why? What's wrong?' she said, shoving the handgun in her pants pocket.

'Shit, he shouldn't have seen you,' said TCG, clenching his teeth; he grabbed his head and swore.

Suddenly, there was a rapid knock on the door. He looked at Liana and put his finger on his lips. Liana went so silent that she could only hear her heart thumping against her chest. Suddenly, somebody repeatedly started banging on the door with their fists; it seemed as if they were trying to break down the door. With trembling hands, TCG turned the key, the metal grating against the lock. The door swung open, revealing a world of uncertainty beyond.

Liana braced herself, ready for whatever awaited them on the other side. The truth was out there, lurking in the shadows, and she was about to face it head-on.

'Ello, I'm Leo, part of the skipper's lot,' Leo announced. 'Got to give the leccy box a once-over right by the blinkin' window,' he said, smiling happily.

His blue crew uniform was crisp, and a badge adorned his chest, displaying his name and face; TCG hesitated, torn between suspicion and protocol, but eventually, he stepped aside, allowing Leo to enter.

Leo hummed to himself as he walked in and approached the window. He noticed that Liana was observing him. 'Having a lovely afternoon?' he said cheerfully.

'Yes, and the sea's so beautiful and marvellous,' stuttered Liana, casually looking at TCG.

Leo fumbled about with some wires in the electric box and tried to start a conversation, 'So, where are you fellows heading?' he asked, feigning casual interest.

TCG's eyes darted towards Liana, a silent plea for her to play along.

'We're going to Isle of Man,' Liana improvised, her mind racing. The lie tasted bitter, but survival demanded it.

Leo became silent and started focusing on his task.

The room seemed to close in; Liana leaned against the wall and continued to observe him.

Leo's hand clenched and unclenched nervously, and TCG's impatience grew; he occupied himself with his phone and started texting.

Liana noticed Leo's hand sinking into his pocket. He pulled his hand back out slowly, and that's when she realised something was terribly wrong; her instincts screamed out danger. 'TCG, he's got a gun!' she yelled.

TCG quickly looked up upon hearing her sudden shriek, his phone still in his hand.

Leo's icy gaze locked on to him; the gun in his hand felt heavy, its cold metal promising to kill on the spot.

'It will be a pleasure shooting you in front of Liana,' his smile was a predator's grin, a wolf baring its sharp teeth.

'Why do you bloody shitheads always like to mess with me?' sighed TCG; he stepped forward, positioned himself between Leo and Liana, and swiftly flicked his gun out.

Leo smirked, 'I don't think that was a good idea, 'cause, with one bullet, I'll take both of you down.'

Liana's instincts kicked in. She sprinted for the door, yanked it open, and ran out of the room. Obviously, like an ordinary girl, she ran to call for help, but as she ran through the corridors, strange shadows pursued her. Two men in black were closing in on her.

The ferry's passengers had no idea what was happening; the captain's announcement had summoned them onto the deck, and they had no clue about the danger lurking below.

Liana's breath came in ragged gasps as she ran through the dimly lit corridor. Her heart thumped hard against her chest, and each beat emphasised the urgency of her escape.

The two men behind her were relentless; their hefty footsteps closed in like a predator on the prowl.

Her pace faltered, her legs aflame, and panic gnawed at her chest. She quickly glanced over her shoulder and saw the two shadows gaining ground.

Dizziness swirled in her head, and her vision blurred at the edges. The corridor was a twisted maze of shadows, the air thick with tension. Her heart pounded against her ribs as she felt a sudden iron grip yanking back her hair.

One of the men grabbed her arm, his fingers digging into her skin, leaving red marks, 'What do you want from me?' Liana's voice trembled as she yelled, desperation lacing her words.

The man's eyes bore into Liana's, a dangerous glint dancing in their depths; his arms encircled her waist, pulling her closer. The chill of his touch sent shivers down her spine, and she wondered if he could feel the fear she was going through. His voice, a low, menacing whisper, brushed against her ear like a blade. 'Why don't you ask TCG? The son of a bastard,' his voice was harsh and threatening. 'He's got the blimey answer floating in his gob.'

Liana really couldn't understand what was going on; she had no clue what the moron was talking about; she hated these guys, including TCG!

Before she could ponder further, a voice boomed through the darkness, 'Get your bloody hands off her!' the words were sharp and stern.

Liana spun her head around and saw TCG charging towards them with blood streaking down his forehead. His dark hair was a mess, and his eyes were blazing with fury. The second man reacted swiftly, pulling a gun out from his pocket.

The shot reverberated through the narrow corridor, and Liana's scream joined the cacophony.

TCG staggered, breathing heavily; the pain from the wound on his right arm was unbearable, a searing reminder of the battle that had just unfolded; his fingers trembled as he touched the wound, and each heartbeat sent fresh waves of agony through his body. He gritted his teeth to stop himself from screaming out loud. His legs threatened to give out, but he pushed forward, seeking revenge; blood dripped from his fingertips, staining the ground crimson.

But hurting TCG was the last thing anyone should do. Anger struck his heart, and fire swam through his blood; he drew out his gun from his leather holster and shot continuously back at the man, each shot sounding like a thunderclap.

The man crumpled and collapsed to the ground with his clothes stained in unforgiving blood.

Liana watched breathlessly as TCG bravely stood his ground. His gaze met hers, and for a fleeting moment, she glimpsed something beyond his cold eyes; the man holding Liana suddenly threw her onto the ground, whipped out his handgun, and pulled the trigger; the deafening crack of the gunshot echoed through the narrow corridor.

The bullet hit TCG, making him stumble back, the unbearable pain in his left shoulder threatening to swallow him whole; his own shot missed its target. It ricocheted off the walls, and the world around him became an uneasy haze.

His breaths came in ragged gasps; he collapsed onto the cold floor. The world around him began to tilt like a ship caught in a storm; his sharp eyes caught sight of Liana's worried face, and memories surged forth when a bullet had skimmed his leg, the unbearable pain crashing against the walls of his mind and body. At that time of pain and agony, Liana had smiled at him, making him feel comfort. He started remembering the warmth of her soft hand that had rested on his shoulder, the curve of her lips when she had smiled, a smile that had made him grin, and her sweet voice that had danced in his ears, a balm for his wounded soul.

And then, like a sudden gust of wind extinguishing a candle, his mind blurred. The memories slipped through his mind, vanishing into the abyss. He clung to them desperately, but they were wisps of smoke slipping away, leaving only an unbearable ache.

But Liana was like a storm. Her comprehensive and unyielding eyes held a reservoir of fury. With a swift motion, she wrenched the gun from her jeans pocket, the same one TCG had given her earlier.

The man's laughter, once carefree and mocking, twisted into a guttural scream, a primal sound wrenched from the depths of his being; the air crackled with tension as the bullet, guided by vengeance, tore through his side, his knees buckled, and he crumpled to the floor.

Liana had no time to lose and ran towards TCG. 'TCG, get up!' she cried.

His blank expression met hers, a question lingering in his eyes. 'Who are you?' he said in a weird tone.

'Don't say that, just get up,' she snapped.

Liana heard footsteps approaching her and found it to be the captain; she stood up quickly with her handgun and looked at the captain straight into his eyes.

The captain's sly eyes bore into hers like a predator assessing its prey. 'I see TCG has finally felt the taste of pain,' laughed the captain. Liana stepped backwards, holding the gun tightly.

'I've felt worse pain than this, and I'm not going to let you make me feel that pain again!' shouted TCG, unexpectedly slowly getting up and taking support from a wall to regain his balance.

'Oh, have you ever told Liana how you felt when you were going through that pain,' smirked the captain. TCG didn't let him say another word and shot the captain in the heart; the corridor echoed with the sharp report of the gunshot. The wounded man staggered, his fingers fumbling for the weapon in his waist holster, but fate had already dealt its hand; he collapsed, hitting his head on the floor and died instantly.

The air hung heavy with tension, and the scent of gunpowder clung to the walls. Adrenaline surged through TCG's body as he limped forward, 'Come on, let's go!' he shouted, staggering up the corridor.

Liana's sharp voice trailed after him: 'Oh, such a relief, you've come back to your bloody senses!'

TRIPLE CASTE GANGSTER

.

Chapter Six
Midnight is clear! A slap forms a tear!

They both sprinted to the deck, where a lively gathering of holidaymakers chatted and laughed. Glasses full of drinks clinked in their hands, children ran around and laughed, while women gossiped and glanced out at the sea, laughing and joking. Men's voices boomed, filling the air with thunderous energy.

TCG pressed his earpiece and spoke madly through them. 'Sergeant Andrew! Quickly, I need backup. They're after me; they were following me all along,' he said, catching his breath.

Andrew's voice remained calm, but an undercurrent of panic and dread seeped through, 'Sure, I'm sending Officer Steven over. He'll be there very soon!'

Liana and TCG hid themselves, seeking refuge in the jam-packed crowds. TCG, who was bloodstained, pulled his hoodie over his head; his gun, concealed in his pocket, weighed heavily. The bullet wound throbbed, a relentless reminder of danger and death. 'Don't worry, Steven's gonna pick us up,' he whispered, glancing towards Liana.

'How is this Steven going to come?' whispered Liana, totally confused and worried.

TCG looked at her, urgency etched on his face, 'He'll be coming to the ferry by speedboat, then we're going to board it and get the shit out of here,' he whispered.

An hour slipped by as they both concealed themselves in the cramped and excited crowds; children's laughter and shouting pierced the air, 'Dolphins, dolphins!' they screamed, jumping up and down on the ferry.

Liana's gaze shifted towards the sea. Her eyes brightened as dolphins jumped together in and out from the vast ocean, whistling happily amongst themselves. Her expression suddenly changed, and her face fell. She wished she had a family who could protect her, not somebody she didn't know. 'I wish my mum was here,' she sighed sadly.

'Why?' smirked TCG. His glossy black eyes glared at her with an intense gaze that sent a shiver down her spine.

'Obviously, you don't know this, but I didn't know that my mum passed away until I was the age of ten. My aunty just didn't mention it to me,' she sighed, feeling a mix of vulnerability and sorrow.

TCG's gaze deepened as he stared into her eyes, his pupils dilated with a hidden longing. His whispered words, as gentle as the summer breeze, wove a delicate tapestry of confusion across her face, 'Your mother didn't simply just pass away like that.'

'What do you mean?' Liana replied, 'I'm not getting what you're trying to say.' Her voice was slightly breathless.

TCG couldn't resist the temptation any longer; with a trembling hand, he gently touched her head; his touch sent shivers down her spine, and he whispered softly in her ear, 'She was murdered,' his soft voice caused electric currents to flow through her veins.

Startled, Liana recoiled, a gasp escaping her lips, 'What on earth are you talking about? You know nothing about my mother!' Her voice trembled, a blend of fear and curiosity.

TCG shrugged his shoulders and stared into the blue sea.

'Keep your assumptions to yourself. Probably that's what happened to your own mum!' she shouted angrily.

TCG frowned deeply, then retorted sharply, 'Shut the hell up!' His smirk betrayed a hint of superiority. Meanwhile, the sun delicately descended on the horizon, its rays painting elongated shadows across the beautiful deck of the ferry.

TCG and Liana, both acutely aware of the hush that had enveloped them, found their senses heightened in the stillness; the ocean breeze carried a hint of salt, and the rhythmic hum of the ferry's engines gave out a peaceful sound.

Suddenly, TCG's grip tightened on Liana's arm, and his eyes darted towards a man who moved with a cunning purpose, weaving through the crowd like a shadow.

Liana followed the direction of his gaze, her heart racing. What was this man up to?

A little girl skipped past TCG. He pulled her sun hat off, perched precariously on her head, and plopped it on Liana's head. An old man standing next to him held a tray of lemonade. TCG grabbed a glass of lemonade off the tray and turned his back on him. The old man shook his head and raised an eyebrow but said nothing and walked off.

The man they were watching halted, his gaze fixed on TCG. Was he after them? TCG took another sip of lemonade, pretending to be calm and relaxed.

Liana leaned closer, her voice barely audible, 'He's watching you,' she murmured. She casually looked at the man and whispered to TCG, 'Yes, he's definitely eyeing you up.'

TCG changed his voice into a loud, heavy voice and spoke to Liana, purposely catching the man's attention. His eyes narrowed, and his voice changed, 'Beautiful is the ocean that surrounds us and amazing are the rivers, which spread their arms out to provide us with fresh water,' he said, acting like a professional person sipping on a glass of lemonade.

On hearing his speech, the man instantly turned away and headed off down the deck.

Liana removed the sun hat from her head, gently placing it back on the girl standing by the railing. Her gaze was fixed on the endless expanse of water, and the child seemed oblivious to the tension around her, lost in her own little world.

'Look over there,' TCG whispered, pointing towards the water, 'There's Steven.'

Liana followed his gaze, spotting a speedboat tearing across the waves. TCG activated his phone torch, signalling to Steven that they'd seen him.

Steven spotted him and manoeuvred the speedboat towards the back side of the ferry, where no people existed. TCG pushed through the thick crowds, with Liana following at his heels.

The ocean churned below, its depths swallowing the sun's fading glow.

TCG's pulse raced as he leaned over the ferry's railing. He looked down into the blue ocean and took a deep breath. Suddenly, a shout disturbed him: 'What do you think you're doing, trying to jump into the deep ocean like a seal?'

He spun around to see whose sharp voice had just thundered through the air. His eyes caught sight of a prideful man doing a hard and unforgiving walk.

'These bloody relentless pests just won't stop trying to catch up to me!' shouted TCG as the man pulled out a knife. The blade caught the last rays of the setting sun, dazzling like a shard of light, with danger etched into the steel.

The man charged, the knife firm and tight in his hand. Liana's scream pierced the air like a siren's wail, but TCG acted swiftly. His hand clamped over her mouth to stop her screaming. His touch sent a jolt through her, a mix of fear and something else she had never felt before. The man started running towards them with a smirk across his face.

'Hold on tight,' commanded TCG, grabbing and lifting her effortlessly.

He quickly but steadily climbed down the ferry's metal safety railing, with Liana clinging to him with fear.

The man started following them down the safety railing, closing in quickly, his eyes locked on TCG's head.

Liana watched in amazement as she realised that TCG was more than action; she wondered what secrets lay hidden in those intense eyes.

The man lunged, knife aimed at TCG's head, but he defied gravity, leaping off the ferry; the howling wind whipped his hair as they plunged towards the sea. The sound of Liana's heart-shattering shriek filled the air.

'You got to be kidding me, ya asshole!' roared the man, looking at TCG jumping off the ferry. 'You won't survive that jump, dumb bastard.'

Liana yelled her head off as she felt herself falling. The wind continued to howl, snatching her screams away. Her hair, a wild cascade of blonde strands, danced like flames in the wind, obscuring her vision.

TCG, the enigmatic figure who had pulled her into this freefall, remained eerily composed. His grip on her arms was unyielding. His wild eyes bore into hers, a silent command to trust him. The intensity of his gaze held her captive as if he could see into the depths of her heart.

TCG's irises were a stormy mix of grey and black, flickering with hidden emotions. 'Hold your breath!' he shouted with sweat trickling down his eyebrow, and as soon as he said those words, Liana felt herself hitting the water.

She sensed water seeping into her hair and up her nose. TCG's grip, once tight, slipped away, leaving her alone in the cold depths.

Liana's strokes cut through the water, each movement fuelled by a desperate need for survival. Her lungs screamed for air, and the world above blurred into a silvery haze. Bubbles escaped from her lips, waltzing upwards in a silent dance. The surface seemed a mere whisper away, yet it eluded her grasp on reality, an ever-distant mirage. As her gaze shifted to the left, she found herself staring at the sinking figure of TCG, who seemed to harbour untold secrets.

Liana stretched her arm out, fingers straining towards him, but the distance between them seemed impossible. The salty water enveloped her, pulling her downward as if the ocean conspired to keep them apart. Her chest tightened, and her lungs craved for air, yet she persisted.

TCG fought against the relentless pull of the ocean; his eyes held a storm of emotions swirling within, his hair danced like seaweed, and his skin took on the same pale translucence as the surrounding waves.

TCG's hand stretched toward hers, their fingers intertwining in a desperate touch against the relentless pull of the sea. The saltwater clung to their skin, a bittersweet reminder of their shared struggle. They bridged the gap, a fragile connection in the vast expanse. TCG stared at her worried eyes, the saltwater clinging to her lashes like unshed tears. He pulled her closer, the weight of the ocean pressing against them.

The waves fought against their bodies, relentless and powerful; as they reached the surface, gasping for air, the sun's rays bore down upon them, turning the water into a beautiful colour of gold liquid.

Liana gasped in a rush of panic and clung to TCG's arms, her fingers digging into his skin, but a rogue wave crashed upon her, wrenching her away. She let go of his arm with panic in her eyes.

TCG lunged forward, his fingers closing around Liana's hand just in time. The saltwater clung to her trembling skin, and he hauled her up, her weight pressing against his shoulders. Her voice was emotional and desperate. 'Don't let go of me,' she pleaded, her head finding refuge on his shoulder. The cold waves snapped at her legs like a predator stalking its prey. TCG held her tightly, fighting the pull of the deep ocean.

Liana felt his grasp slipping away from her arms. She let out a heart-aching shriek, her voice filled with fear and longing, 'Keep holding onto me!' She tightened her grip around his waist and choked on the water that seeped into her mouth.

The taste of salt and fear lingered in the air as the waves continued their relentless assault. TCG brushed the wet hair out of her face, his lips close to her ear, and the sound of water carrying his whispered promise, 'Hold onto me and don't worry, I won't let you go.'

But the ocean had other plans. Another wave roared above them, pulling Liana under. TCG swam towards her, clawing at the powerful currents. He encircled his arms around her waist. His strength waned, and they sank deeper, yet he held on, fingers intertwined, their life on the brink of chaos.

Liana became motionless. The water, the waves, everything started fading. Her focus remained on TCG's determined and unwavering eyes.

A huge wave crashed over them and tore their hands apart again, wrenching them from each other's grasp. The force of it left them disoriented and suspended in the chaos of salt and foam. Liana, her chest heaving, fought to regain her bearings. Her eyes, wide and desperate, settled upon him. His silhouette blurred through the churning water, a lone figure equally adrift.

Liana looked worriedly at him, seeking help, but he sharply tore his eyes away from her, his jaw clenched tightly. He averted his face, concealing his emotions.

Liana tried to swim to him, but the heavy waves crashed down on her. TCG remained motionless as if paralysed. He didn't reach for her or fight against the pull of the deep as if she were nothing but part of the sea.

Her blonde hair spread around her like a sunlit halo, catching the sunlight filtering through the water.

The world became surreal, colours seemed hard to recognise, and sounds became muffled. Her senses switched off one by one, leaving only the dreadful sensation of sinking.

In that suspended moment, Liana wondered if she'd ever resurface; perhaps this was where she belonged, submerged, weightless, lost in the hidden depths. And as the darkness enveloped her, she realised that life was precious and short!

'Ouch! Don't treat my wound so roughly. And yeah, you just watch what I'm going to do with you when I get better. I'm going to make sure you walk off without an arm!'

'Here you go, I'm all done. You sure got banged out. I haven't seen you like this in a long while. I mean, the last time this happened to you was when…,'

'When I got involved with MY MASHED-UP FAMILY!'

An eerie light seeped into Liana's eyes as she heard the sudden shout. Was she dreaming, or was she actually breathing in the cool air? She moved her fingers, slowly and steadily lifting her hand; she felt like water was stuck in her throat and let out a soft cough.

'You're awake,' Liana saw a man with ginger hair and bubbly green eyes approaching her. 'How are you feeling? You seem cold,' he said, smiling. He lifted a blanket over her shoulders and walked off.

After pondering for a while and swimming in deep thoughts, Liana decided to get up. She sat up and felt cold air around her neck. 'Hold on, where do you think you're going?' smiled the same man she had seen before. 'Here, have this. It'll make you feel better,' he said, giving her a hot drink.

Liana sipped on it slowly, and the man remained standing, staring at the night sky, 'My name's Steven, Officer Steven, actually,' he laughed.

'So, you're the lunatic who scooped us out?' she whispered.

'Pardon me!' Steven responded. Liana turned her face away from him and found TCG sitting on the far end of the speedboat, lying on his back and staring at the starry night. Liana frustratedly turned her face away from him and looked at her hands.

'I know it was a big day for an ordinary girl like you,' smiled Steven.

'I'm not an ordinary girl,' she said, raising her voice and staring at him directly in the eyes.

'You're a bit…em, how's your hand? It looks a bit hurt,' he said, changing the topic.

'Why should I tell you how I feel?' she yelled, tears filling her eyes.

Steven sighed, walked over to his seat, and started fumbling around for a while before returning to Liana. 'Here, this will help,' he said, putting a hot water bottle on her hand.

She felt the heat warming her hand, and her body started feeling much better. 'Thanks,' she sighed solemnly.

'You're welcome,' he smiled, walking over to his seat.

A robotic voice suddenly spoke, 'Would you still like to have your speedboat on automatic?'

'Yes, Robo Stella,' said Steven, looking out at the sea.

The noise of water splashing reverberated throughout the cool night. The glowing moon, a luminescent lantern, cast its enchanting glow upon the restless sea, each ripple becoming a brushstroke of magic, painting the waves in hues of silver and indigo. The stars dazzled the sky, their brilliance looking like the finest gemstones you'll ever find; they adorned the vast canvas of the sky, a celestial mosaic.

Peace and tranquillity filled the chilly breeze, and then, rising from the depths, came the beautiful melody, the song of the blue whales. Their voices danced through the waves, filling the ocean with eloquence and peace.

Steven looked at Liana from the corner of his eye as she got up and slowly walked towards TCG. He smiled to himself and hummed happily.

Liana approached TCG with a hushed reverence and stood still with her back leaning on the side of the speedboat. His eyes were veiled in darkness, his hair flowed upon his face, and his hands were behind his head like usual as he rested peacefully.

'TCG,' she whispered.

His eyes shot open, and he stared straight at the peaceful sky above.

'TCG, are you all right?' she asked.

A strange laugh escaped within him, stabbing her heart, his voice a mere whisper, 'All right, after what's happened to me?'

'Don't blame me,' she sighed, a note of weariness in her voice.

'Everything that has happened to me is your fault,' he smirked.

'Shut up, you're the one that decided to take me home!' Liana said, raising her voice and giving him dirty looks.

'Did you tell me to shut up? You daft cow!' he yelled, suddenly sitting up.

'Yes, I did, and I'm saying it straight in your face. Shut the heck up!' shouted Liana, her sharp words ignited the air between them.

In a swift and furious moment, TCG's hand shot up, striking Liana across the face with hatred. The force of the blow sent her flying onto the floor. Steven, silently observing the commotion, quickly came running and positioned himself between TCG and Liana.

'Are you out of your mind, TCG? We're in the middle of the ocean. We don't want anything going wrong!' Steven shouted.

Liana's crying echoed in TCG's ears, increasing his wrath, 'Steven, don't get involved, or else I'll throw you off the boat!' bellowed TCG.

Steven knew it would be better for him if he stayed quiet.

'Liana, you better shut your mouth!' shouted TCG, glaring at her, his eyes ablaze with ferocity.

Overcome with emotion, Liana couldn't stop herself from crying. She stomped off to where she was sitting before. Suddenly pausing, she turned, her gaze piercing TCG. She yelled out, 'I hate you! You've never said my name before, and when you flippin' did, you said it out of so much hatred. Ya piece of shit!'

Chapter Seven
Get the heck to London! Traps come sudden!

TCG stared at the stars and sighed. Their distant glimmer reflected in his pupils like shards of ice. The chilly breeze swept through the air, ruffling his long black hair and revealing a scar that snaked across his temple. His lips were pressed into a thin line. He was a man who held secrets darker than the night itself.

The constellations' reflection twirled within his irises, transforming them into feline orbs that hungered not for mere prey but for something that his heart desired. The night, a celestial tapestry, wove shadows with threads of moonlight, concealing secrets in its quietude.

TCG felt a warm hand rest on his shoulder. He turned, and there stood Steven.

Steven's eyes held unspoken emotions, and then he finally spoke, with his hand still resting on TCG's shoulder, 'I see your pain,' he murmured, 'No one has experienced the path you've walked on. I fully understand.' TCG sighed and pushed Steven's hand away, 'But listen,' he continued, 'Don't shatter her heart.'

Steven's words weighed heavy on TCG's heart. Suddenly, he turned away. His footsteps receded, fading into the night, leaving TCG with a heart that was both heavy and broken.

The sun's bright rays twinkled on the seashore, inviting a new day to the busy and frantic world; seagulls screeched above the clouds, and the noise of cargo ships getting ready to sail filled the warm air. Fishermen in sunhats settled into their boats, anticipating the day's catch, and the melody of the waves splashing in the blue sea filled everyone's ears with nature's natural song.

'We've arrived!' Steven exclaimed joyously, shielding his eyes from the sun's glare and peering eagerly towards the harbour, 'Hey, do you remember the last time I was here, I held a sandwich in my hand, and a seagull swooped down and snatched it right out of my hand, after that I looked up to see where it had gone, and that silly seagull pooped all over my face?' laughed Steven with TCG joining in the laughter.

'It looked like you had white paint poured on top of you,' said TCG, laughing his head off.

'Ah, those carefree childhood days!' giggled Steven, but he fell silent when he saw Liana's grumpy face. She had been quiet since dawn, barely touching her food.

TCG continued joking around with Steven, but Steven stopped laughing and, in a gentle tone, addressed Liana. 'Hey, Liana. Did you enjoy the sea?' he asked, smiling warmly.

'No, Officer, I didn't. I wish I had my mum with me to hold my hand and comfort me, and my dad, I wish I could tell him how bad people have treated me,' she said, looking at the port before her.

'You've had a tough life, girl, but that's what's unique about you,' Steven said softly, his voice tinged with empathy, 'you jump off, girl, TCG will be right behind you.'

With a nod, Liana jumped onto the wooden planks and walked onto the harbour; she glanced backwards and saw Steven whispering in TCG's ear.

TCG nodded and then jumped onto the wooden planks; he approached Liana and said, 'Come on, let's get going.'

'Sure, you get going. Get out of my face right now. I'll go home from here myself,' said Liana, walking off.

TCG sighed and followed her; his frustration was evident as he watched her storm off with attitude and pride. 'Excuse me, we're in Scotland,' he said, 'I don't know how you're going to go all the way to your house by yourself. It's bloody in London!'

TCG's anger overwhelmed him, and he yelled, 'You know what? Get out of here, and let's see how you cope with everything!'

Liana smirked and continued walking, but as soon as she was out of TCG's sight, she sighed heavily. She had no clue what to do as she roamed aimlessly.

Just when tears threatened to spill out, a woman caught her attention.

She was wearing a leather jacket, and her red nails were a stark contrast against the black outfit she wore. She started staring at Liana as if she were a lost five-year-old. 'Keen for a haun?' she asked, speaking in a gentle and soft tone, 'Ye look a bit scunnered, and it's nae guide bein' a' by yer ain sel.'

Liana hesitated upon hearing her Scottish accent. She had once heard some teenagers talking in a heavy Scottish accent at her university and had learned a bit from some Scottish girls, so now the time had come to put her communication skills into action, 'Aye, that'd be braw,' she stuttered, trying to find her tongue.

'Whaur dae ye need tae gang?' the woman asked with a smile.

Liana hesitated, her heart a compass pointing towards distant horizons. 'Weel,' she finally confessed, 'I'm aff tae London, think ye could point me tae the train station?'

The woman's eyes widened, 'Aye, it's a fair trek indeed!' Her enthusiasm was funny, 'Ah, dinnae fash yersel', laddie! I'll tak' a wee dander tae the train station, It's nae a braw lang trek frae here, ye ken.'

Liana's jaws dropped. She had no clue what the woman had just said, but she started following her towards her car, relieved upon finding some help. The woman opened the passenger car door, 'Wor lass, tek a seat,' she said, her smile reassuring. She shut the door behind Liana as she jumped inside. The woman then walked over to the driver's side, got in, and started driving.

The woman remained silent throughout the drive, which made Liana feel a bit nervous, but something about her presence seemed to ease her nerves. As they turned into a dimly lit alley, the car suddenly stopped.

Liana's pulse quickened. 'This is not a train station,' she protested, eyes scanning the shadows.

'Who said Ah'm takin' ye tae the train station?' the woman laughed, jumping out of the car and striding towards the passenger door. She hurriedly swung the door open, yanking Liana out of the vehicle, her grip unyielding; she held Liana's arms tightly behind her back and kept on pushing her forward until they reached a black door; it loomed over them. The word 'Office' was etched into it in bold letters.

The woman unlocked it effortlessly, never releasing Liana's hands. Liana was made to walk up a dull, narrow corridor that stretched before them, lined with ominous doors. Each one seemed to hold dark secrets and a whispered promise of danger. The woman knocked on one of the doors, and a man's voice answered, 'Who is it?'

'It's me, Blood Beauty,' she declared proudly. 'Open up, Fang.' Liana cringed upon hearing the woman's horrible name, and fear tightened its grip on her heart as the door swung open.

'Come in, come in. I was hoping to hear from you,' said Fang happily, with a sinister smile playing on his lips as Blood Beauty walked in with utmost pride shining on her face. Fang's laughter echoed through the dimly lit room, a chilling undertone beneath his smirk.

His sleek black hair flowed past his ears, and his grey eyes held evil desires. As they bore into Liana's soul, a shiver raced down her spine; when he spoke, his voice was a velvet blade slicing through the air with a promise of long-awaited reckoning. 'Ah,' he murmured, 'You've brought me a gift, haven't you? One I've hungered for.'

He stood up from his chair and walked over to Blood Beauty, 'Take her to my main office, and as I promised, you will be greatly rewarded,' he whispered in a low, barely audible voice.

The woman barged off with Liana, grabbing her brutally by the arms; she strode off down the hallway and shoved her into a lift. Liana knew she was being taken underground; they started descending into the bowels of the Earth.

The lift doors opened, revealing an underground car park vast enough to swallow huge areas.

Liana stumbled out, disoriented; the air smelled of dampness and secrets.

Blood Beauty's grip tightened, tough as iron.

Liana tried to wriggle free by kicking Blood Beauty in her shin, but she had her tightly gripped. Blood Beauty grabbed her by the jaws and laughed in her face, 'Ah, lassie, ye're gonnae be a right deid meat, hen!' her voice dripping of venom.

She shoved Liana into a Bimmer, a sleek, polished metal beast, and locked her in, leaving her staring after her like a caged bird.

She sat for a long time in the Bimmer like a disowned girl. Suddenly, a broad man jumped in the driver's seat. He said nothing, and his eyes were hidden behind dark shades.

The engine roared to life, and the car surged forward. Liana's reflection stared back at her from the window, a captive bird with wings clipped, and dreams shattered.

She stared out of the car window, her heart feeling heavy.

Each street unfolded like a chapter in the dreaded drive, a relentless narrative of twists and turns. Motorways merged, their lanes mazed, leading deeper into chaos.

Her heart clung to the memory of TCG, a bittersweet ache that twisted within her. She wished she had never left him. She replayed their last moments together in her mind. The gangster voice, the way he looked at her, it all haunted her now. If only she hadn't walked away and stayed by his side, perhaps she wouldn't be entangled in this mind-blowing mess of regret and longing.

The man parked smoothly in a parking lot and jumped out of the car like a posh guy on an important job. 'Get out!' he said, yanking her by the arm.

Skyscrapers loomed above her, their glass structures looking dull and miserable.

Liana got shoved around all the way through a gigantic and stunning skyscraper. 'Get in the lift now, you daft bitch!' yelled the man, getting impatient with her stubbornness and attitude.

The man's voice sliced through the air like a sharp blade, 'Come on, you cow, shift yer bloody self outta the lift, will ya? Do I have to spell it out for ya, step by step?' he shouted, his impatience hanging heavy. He made her walk up a long, quiet corridor that seemed like the walls were whispering secrets.

He walked up to a door, and with a decisive swing, it yielded, revealing a room adorned with richness and bling.

Like frozen constellations, crystal chandeliers hung from the ceiling, their prismatic facets casting fractured rainbows across the vast polished marble below. Liana's eyes darted around; she might as well have stepped into a rich man's dreamscape. The mahogany desk stood like an ancient altar, its polished surface reflecting her fear.

He left her in the posh and elegant room, leaving her gaping around in astonishment. Then, the doors behind her swung open, and to her surprise, Fang entered. Clearly, he had arrived in another vehicle. His grey eyes held secrets darker than the deep ocean.

'Hi, Liana,' he said in an eerie tone, 'Are you shocked seeing me again?'

'What do you want from me?' she yelled.

Fang circled her like a predator, ready to pounce on its prey. 'Haven't you ever looked at your reflection before? If you had, you probably would know!' he smiled, walking towards a posh chair and sitting down. 'You represent someone.'

'Why do you guys want to kill me?' her voice trembled with utmost fear.

Fang blinked, his voice chilling, 'Kill? Why would I want to kill you?' he whispered.

'That's what you've been trying to do all this time,' Liana scoffed.

Fang leaned back in the chair, his fingers tracing invisible patterns on the armrest, 'No, no,' he said, his voice a low murmur, 'you're getting the story wrong. I don't want to kill you, but Black Hawk's party wants to kill you,' he sighed.

'Why do they want to kill me, and what do you want from me?' she shouted impatiently.

'Patience,' Fang replied, his eyes flickered towards the window, 'TCG killed Black Hawk's only son. A debt of blood has to be paid, they say, so they want revenge back by killing you in front of him.'

Liana's brow furrowed, 'Everything I just heard from your gob doesn't make any sense.'

'And yeah, I want to kill TCG in front of you,' laughed Fang, standing up with an evil grin spread across his face.

Liana laughed at Fang and smirked, 'TCG means nothing to me, and I don't mean anything to him, you jerk!'

Chapter Eight
Hear the gunshot! Bang... who's it got!

'Do you recall when you were sitting on the bench just before TCG came?' Fang's voice was low; his fingers drummed an ominous rhythm on the armrest.

Her eyes snapped shut as she was dragged back into the past, 'Yes, I do,' she whispered, a shiver running down her spine.

Fang leaned in, his voice a growl, 'Well, the guy that jumped out of the black Merc was one of my fellow men, and he got killed. That gives me another excuse to kill TCG, and the main reason I want him dead...I'll tell you some other time!'

'Yes, I do expect you to kill him, do as you please, and if you don't mind me asking, who was the guy with the cap?' said Liana.

A cruel smirk twisted Fang's lips. 'He was one of Black Hawks men; he didn't get far, did he?' His laughter was a sinister echo in the dim room.

Liana's gaze dropped, a curtain of blonde hair veiling her face; then, with a swift motion, she locked eyes with Fang, her voice like a calm storm, 'You or the Black Hawk's party can do whatever you want; I've got nothing to lose.'

Fang laughed, his eyes narrowing, 'You're a strange girl! I certainly don't understand you!' he exclaimed, looking at her annoyed; a knock on the door interrupted his speech. 'Who is it?'

'Boss, it's urgent. Kevin Lee wants to talk to you,' a gruff voice answered from outside the door.

Fang grinned, his teeth glinting like daggers, 'Bring him up. It will be a pleasure speaking to him,' he smiled.

'Are you going to keep the girl with you?' asked the man.

'Of course!' he replied, rolling his grey fox eyes.

Moments later, Kevin Lee arrived; he was tall and skinny, and a smile spread across his pale face.

As he stepped through the doorway, his gaze latched onto Liana, wide-eyed and piercing, as though he'd seen a ghost.

'Hi, William Archer,' smiled Kevin, using Fang's actual name in a dangerous game of familiarity.

Fang met his stare, a cold smirk creeping across his face, 'No one addresses me by my real name! Do you hear me?'

'Same applies to me,' replied Kevin, the air crackled with unspoken threats.

'Let's get to business. Why have you come?' Fang ordered, his voice slicing through the tension.

'You know why I have come, half a million, and we get the diamond,' exclaimed Kevin.

Fang's laughter was a low rumble, 'The diamond is not worth that much.'

'I was afraid you might say that, but I don't blame you. You've gone through many problems getting this diamond. What about a million then?' laughed Kevin. Liana observed the two men; she did not know what they were talking about, but she could only understand that they were talking very indirectly.

Fang smiled, 'Deal.'

The snap of Kevin's briefcase echoed like a gunshot as he presented the contents with a flourish.

Liana's eyes narrowed, scrutinising Kevin's attire. His thick black gloves bore a distinctive emblem: a hawk in mid-strike. With a heavy heart, she realised he was one of the black hawk's men!

Liana was escorted out of the enormous skyscraper, her steps shadowed by Kevin Lee's silent presence.

Under the dimming sky, the car park felt eerily deserted. This time, her escort directed her to a different vehicle, its windows tinted in dark, impenetrable black.

He drove off with her onto another motorway. The cityscape blurred past, a cascade of lights and shadows. Liana's destination remained a mystery. The building they approached loomed above her, holding dark secrets and evilness.

But this time, she felt calm instead of worried; she didn't know what was happening; she just felt disowned and confused.

The room was dark and cold, the air weirdly stuffy, and voices of mockery and laughter filled the air. However, a girl with stubbornness and attitude stood in the centre of the room, not caring what people would say to her. She cast a nervous gaze upward, where a ring of metal loomed. From the balcony, faces peered down, some with curiosity, others with mockery and disbelief.

The unforgiving silence suddenly shattered. Black Hawk emerged from the shadows, his presence chilling and dangerous. 'Liana, would you like to say your last words to TCG before I end your life?' he laughed, his voice a serpent's hiss.

Her response was like a blade, sharp and unwavering, 'No, I've got nothing to do with him,' she said, giving Black Hawk daggers.

A cruel laugh erupted from Black Hawk's throat, 'OK, then, but he'll defo be seeing you get shot on camera,' a smirk appeared on his face, 'He killed my brother, then I killed someone very close to him, which I don't want to talk about at this moment because your heart will shatter before I even kill you. Then he killed my nineteen-year-old son six years ago, and now I'll finally be getting my revenge.'

'You're an evil man,' smirked Liana, 'How far do you think you're going to get by doing all this?'

'It's not evil what I'm doing. I chose to leave the American army and build my own army to seek true justice,' sighed Black Hawk, clearly telling a blatant lie.

The gun rose, aligning with Liana's brow, his finger tensed on the trigger. She braced for the end, tears veiling her vision. A trigger was pressed, a bullet sailed through the charged air, and a sudden scream pierced the space.

Liana's eyes shot open. The room was cloaked in shadows and the air smelt of gunpowder.

Her eyes adjusted to the dim light to see Black Hawk sprawled on the floor, blood dripping from his wounded arm, staining the floor.

His gun had slid an arm's length away from him; he lifted his head to the sound of someone calling Liana's name.

'I know you're here, Triple Caste Gangster!' he roared.

Liana looked up, and her gaze darted towards Steven. His eyes were wide with fear and determination. He was holding a lethal firearm, its cold steel promising retribution.

He looked at her worriedly and pointed the firearm towards Black Hawk.

Without warning, a man ran towards Steven and struck him in the face with a powerful roundhouse kick. Steven staggered for a brief moment, and the firearm slipped from his grasp. It plummeted to the ground, and the air seemed to shudder as the weapon collided with the floor, the metallic clang reverberating through the space. Steven talentedly grabbed his opponent by his hair, continuously punching him in the face. The man fell to the floor but managed to get up quickly. He then lunged at Steven, kneeing him in the chest, causing him to stumble into the wall. The balcony became their battleground, a dance of brutality.

Liana's pulse quickened; she needed answers; where was TCG? The one who haunted her nightmares.

Her eyes darted around, but there was no sign of him; Black Hawk picked himself up, his arm bleeding.

His eyes bore into Liana's, a twisted mix of malice and desperation; he grabbed his gun from the floor and swung it into Liana's face, causing it to slash her lip and bleed.

The blood trickled down the side of her face, staining her T-shirt. She staggered backwards with tears blurring her vision. Black Hawk put his finger on the trigger and aimed it at her.

'Oh, no, you don't!' came a sudden voice.

Black Hawk pulled the trigger, but the stranger's intervention defied his wishes. He twisted Black Hawk's arms around his neck and yanked him backwards, causing the bullet to miss Liana by inches.

'TCG! You're here!' screamed Liana, her voice full of utmost relief.

Black Hawk fought for survival, desperation fuelling his veins, but TCG held him in a vice-like grip, slamming him to the ground. They grappled for a while. Eventually, he twisted the gun out of Black Hawk's hand.

TCG's eyes bore into Black Hawk's soul, 'Today,' he hissed, 'I'm going to kill my biggest enemy. Ya should have thought twice before pissing around with the gangster!' he shouted, shooting him straight in the head and three times in the chest.

Meanwhile, on the other side of the hall, Steven flung his adversary over the balcony. Unfortunately for him, more enemies started to appear after hearing the sudden commotion. In a swift, adrenaline-fueled motion, Steven snatched up his sleek, matte-black automatic firearm. The cold metal nestled into his palm, its heavy weight familiar and reassuring. Without hesitation, he pulled the trigger and started firing, blasting anyone who tried to confront him.

The air smelt of gunpowder, and there was chaos everywhere. 'Quickly, TCG, let's get out of here before more of these bastards come!' shouted Steven at the top of his lungs.

TCG grabbed Liana's hand. The ground beneath them quivered with intense fighting; he yanked her towards himself and started running.

And then a sudden shriek echoed through the humid air, 'Dad, Dad!'

TCG spun around, and his eyes caught sight of a teenage girl running towards Black Hawk's dead body. Her eyes, brown like forgotten memories, bore into TCG's soul.

'Dad, are you all right?' she gasped, falling onto her knees. He saw tears running down her face. She stared at TCG with her soft eyes and then grabbed Black Hawk's hand, her voice piercing through the humid air, 'Dad!'

TCG paused and looked at the girl. She reminded him of someone, but he couldn't exactly remember; her tears flowed down her cheeks and onto her dad's hand.

'Come on, TCG, we must get out of here!' Steven shouted, running up to him.

TCG and Liana started sprinting with all their might. Suddenly, he felt Liana's hand slip out of his hand. He spun around and noticed Kevin yanking Liana backwards. Kevin then smashed his phone into her nose, causing blood to spurt out.

TCG gave a hard spinning back kick straight into Kevin's side. Then, with immense anger burning inside him, he flung a hammer punch into his face, followed by a powerful flying knee strike, sending him flying backwards.

TCG pulled Liana to her feet. Her face was painted in blood.

'Come on, we need to go!' he yelled, his command thundering through the darkness as he started running through the building.

Liana's heart raced as she stumbled over an unseen obstacle. Her foot hit a metal pole, and she plummeted towards the unforgiving floor. Time slowed, and the air thickened with dread and fear. The ground rushed up to meet her, and Liana braced for impact. But then, strong arms encircled her, lifting her effortlessly. TCG held her close, breathing heavily. His touch was firm yet oddly gentle, as if he cradled something precious.

Liana's pulse hammered in her ears. She glanced up and caught a glimpse of his face through her blurred vision, a mask of determination etched with concern.

Liana felt darkness seeping into her mind, and old memories started clawing at her consciousness. She gasped and whispered a plea: 'I want mum,' she murmured, reaching for an invisible hand. 'Mummy, hold my hand! Please, Mummy!'

She heard Steven yelling as he sprinted alongside TCG. 'I think she's going to switch off,' he bellowed in a loud, desperate voice. 'That bang in the nose was very severe!'

Liana's vision locked onto TCG and Steven, their movements a frantic blur, sprinting, guns blazing, but then, a shroud of darkness descended, swallowing her world whole. Her consciousness wavered like a flickering candle, and the dark abyss claimed her.

'I don't want to tell her. She probably might kill me.'

'I know it is a bit tricky! I can't really advise you on what to say to her.'

'All that time, I thought she knew; she must be so confused.'

Liana's eyes slowly opened as water trickled into her mouth, making her choke; she started coughing uncontrollably. A man with brown hair and hazelnut eyes looked at her, holding a bottle of water. His spiky hair defied gravity, and his smile was very peculiar. Liana slowly got up and realised she was sitting in the back of a car.

'Rise and shine, girl,' he declared, 'it works every time.'

'Where am I?' she whispered to herself.

'Oh, goody, she's awake!' smiled Steven, twisting his head around to see Liana.

'Oh no, the pest is awake!' TCG's laughter echoed, but there was something sinister in it, a hint of something darker, as he drove madly through the hectic roads.

'She's a quiet girl,' the man with the bottle of water observed, smiling gently.

'No, Joseph,' Steven interjected, his voice gentle, 'She's not quiet; she's just sinking in everything that just happened.'

Liana's anger erupted like a volcano, 'Yes, I'm thinking about how cowardly and stupid you guys are!' Her words were like volcanic ash, scorching everything in their path.

'Oh, there she goes again,' sighed TCG; he knew her too well, and the scars of their shared past ran deep.

'And who's this clown sitting here?' she asked angrily, pointing at Joseph.

'Hey, girl,' Joseph muttered, 'I'm the one that was waiting in the car whilst TCG and Steven went on their mission to save you.'

'I don't think walking away from me was a good idea. Do you remember?' TCG's laughter turned bitter. His eyes locked with Liana's, a silent challenge.

'Shut up! You should have never come back for me; then, at least, I wouldn't need to see your face again!' Liana shouted, clenching her fists and causing her nails to dig into her palm.

'You just wait and see,' TCG's voice dropped to a dangerous whisper, 'you're going to find out what I'm going to do with you when we arrive at our destination.'

Everything in the car went still and quiet, and only the noise of the heavy car engine rumbled in everyone's ears. Steven put the windows down, letting in the cool breeze. The sound of birds happily tweeting could be heard in the distance.

TCG felt Liana's eyes on him, drilling into his back like sharp knives; he didn't look back. Instead, he pressed harder on the gas pedal, driving towards an uncertain future.

'We're here at last!' said Joseph cheerfully, shattering the tension and opening the door.

'Let's get going, I'm proper pooped,' sighed Steven.

Liana followed, her legs feeling heavy and her heart bruised as she followed them towards the entrance of the opulent hotel. Rest awaited her, but revenge burned hotter. She longed to punch TCG, to make him feel even a fraction of her pain. But for now, she was walking towards uncertainty.

'A cup of coffee will do good for me. I've had such a crazy day,' Joseph sighed, his voice a weary echo; the thought of caffeine was a lifeline for him, a desperate attempt to regain strength.

'Hey, what did you do that you had such a crazy day?' questioned Steven, laughing crazily.

'I don't really know,' Joseph chuckled, rubbing his head, 'All I can remember is babysitting the car!'

'Oh, what a great job,' replied Steven sarcastically.

'Is everything set for tomorrow's flight?' TCG inquired.

'Absolutely,' Steven affirmed, a nod emphasising his readiness. 'Tickets, passports, the whole shebang.'

Liana ignored them and stormed into a nearby room. She slammed the door shut, kicked her shoes off, and jumped into a comfortable-looking bed. The mattress cradled her weariness, and she buried her face into the soft pillow.

As sleep enveloped her, dreams swirled like a tornado of memories and regrets. The day's horrors replayed in a ceaseless loop, each scene etched into her mind. TCG's face haunted her continuously.

She wanted to swear at him, to scream and scream until her voice gave out, but for now, she surrendered to the darkness, seeking solace in oblivion.

Tomorrow would bring new battles and fresh scars. The mere thought of flying back to America made her stomach turn. Yet, for now, in the quietness of the hotel room, she slept, a temporary respite in a world gone mad!

Chapter Nine
Shattered pride! Ride the tide!

The lounge hung heavy with unspoken tension, the air thickened by secrets and shared danger. Steven and Joseph, heads bent over their phones, seemed to find peace in the glow of their screens. Liana's gaze moved from one person to another as she walked into the room, her mind uncertain.

Joseph looked up and smiled. 'Need anything?' he asked cheerfully. Liana shook her head, unable to control the storm raging within her. She sat on the windowsill and stared out. Black Hawk's attack had shaken her; she felt as if the purpose of her survival was holding onto a fragile thread.

TCG, the enigmatic protector, had whisked her away to this unfamiliar place he called home. She was brought to his house after nearly getting killed, and now she didn't know what to do; thoughts filled her head: I've got no family to go to. Shall I call the police? How can I do that when two police officers sit beside me? Why do people want to kill me? What will happen next in my life?

TCG walked in with powerful strides. He flung his gun across the glass table, creating a noise that echoed like a thunderclap throughout the room. He lay on the sofa opposite Steven and Joseph, putting his hands behind his head and stretching like a tired cat. 'It looks like you had a long day,' Steven observed, his smile gentle. TCG's laughter held a hint of bitterness.

'Sure, it was hectic,' he laughed, side-eyeing Liana, who was still looking out the window. Had she traded one danger for another? 'Have you checked what I told you to check?' asked TCG, looking back at Steven.

'Yeah, I even told the head office to check; they said it's all clear,' sighed Steven.

Joseph's earpiece started beeping; he pressed the flashing button, his voice businesslike: 'What's cracking?' His eyes widened as he listened on. 'Oh, yes... I see. Tell him I'll be right there in a jiffy,' Joseph stood up. 'They need me in the head office. See you soon,' he smiled and marched off with his usual bouncy walk as if he were just about to do a cartwheel. He left the room, leaving a bubbly atmosphere behind him.

'I spoke to Andrew about opening the new office in Tampa Bay,' Steven announced, his gaze flickering between TCG and Liana. TCG's silence was like a silent storm brewing on the horizon. His eyes locked onto Liana as if she held the answers to unspoken questions. Liana, oblivious, brushed her hair back and stared at the ceiling, lost in her thoughts.

'TCG!' Steven hissed, but TCG remained unmoved, his focus unyielding.

'What?' snapped TCG.

'What are you thinking about?' asked Steven, staring at TCG.

'How will it help if you know what I'm thinking?' he sighed.

Steven looked back at his phone again and frowned, 'That's strange. I didn't select that,' he muttered.

Liana rose and started to walk forward calmly. She reached for the lounge door, ready to escape the charged atmosphere. TCG's loud voice immediately stopped her in her mission.

'Hey, Liana, where are you going?' he asked, sitting up, his eyes narrowing.

'What is it to you?' smirked Liana.

'Oi, this isn't your house, so don't talk like that to me, and even if it was, you still don't have the right to talk to me with such a bad attitude!' shouted TCG.

'Get a life, you moron, and don't talk to me ever again!' Liana hissed, flinging the door open, but TCG's rage followed her. He grabbed his gun from the glass table and flung it at her.

The impact sent shockwaves through her side, forcing her to turn around, 'You jerk!' she shrieked, retrieving the gun from the floor.

'You better not throw that back at me, or I'll show you what I'm going to do to you next!' shouted TCG. His threat echoed a dangerous promise.

'I'm not going to, and anyway, it didn't hurt me!' yelled Liana, anger striking her heart.

'What hurts then?' he yelled, standing up, 'Go on, tell me!' he screamed, marching up to her.

'Come on, bro, calm down,' sighed Steven, glancing at him nervously.

TCG spun around and looked at Steven, 'You shut your mouth before I come and bang you out!' he shouted. Steven fell silent and stared at Liana, hardly blinking at all.

Liana tried to walk out the door, but TCG's looming figure stood before her. 'Tell me right now!' His sharp demand echoed off the walls.

'Tell you what?' said Liana, nearly bursting into tears. She threw the gun across the room, and then her eyes suddenly burst like an overflowing dam, 'I hate you! Now let me go!' she cried, her vulnerability hanging in the air, a fragile plea.

TCG stood out of her way, and she barged off, crying her face off, 'She really must hate me!' he smirked, looking at Steven.

'You need to get a life. You don't understand girls, do you?' shouted Steven, standing up.

'Are you bloody shouting at me?' TCG's voice crackled with tension. His eyes locked onto Steven, and the air thickened, charged with emotion and defiance. He dared Steven to flinch or even make a move.

Steven's response was a weary sigh. He was a middle person in the simmering conflict. 'Yes, I am shouting at you,' he said, brushing past TCG and heading down the hallway.

'Where are you going?' shouted TCG, annoyed by Steven's sudden unusual remark.

'I'm going out so you can have some time to yourself. I think you know what I'm talking about. Don't ya?' he said, walking off.

TCG walked through the hallway, the walls pressing in on him. He slowly walked into the backroom, craving solitude.

He leaned against the cool surface of the wall, pressing his palm onto his temple. His mind swirled like a whirlpool of regret, longing, and unanswered questions, and the weight of Liana's absence bore down on him, an unshakable burden. In the hush of that moment. He pondered, was understanding girls ever truly attainable?

Meanwhile, Liana ran to the back garden and flung herself on the soft grass. 'Why is everyone treating me like I'm not worthy of anything?' she cried out, the desperation evident in her voice as she curled up and held her knees tightly. Her tears created a glistening trail upon the vibrant green grass.

A bird tweeted on a nearby tree, its melodic sound piercing through her sadness. Liana looked up, her eyes shining with a mix of longing and admiration, 'I wish I were like you, free from all troubles,' she whispered, wiping away her tears with a delicate touch.

The gentle wind ruffled her hair, and the sunlight bestowed a golden halo upon her, enfolding her in a tender embrace.

In that moment, Liana's mind drifted back to her childhood, where she would often sing with a sweet yet melancholic voice, a bittersweet release for her sorrows. Liana pushed aside her grief and sang softly, lost in her memories. She temporarily forgot about everything around her and immersed herself in another world.

Unbeknownst to her, TCG heard her voice and raised his head; he couldn't resist the irresistible force that pulled him towards her beautiful voice.

He walked quietly through the hallway, approaching the back sliding glass doors. He looked out and saw Liana lying on the grass; her beautiful voice echoed in the garden's stillness. He stood there quietly and listened intently to her melodic lament.

After a while, he quietly entered the garden, the noise of his footsteps muffled by the soft earth; she remained blissfully unaware of his approach, lost in her thoughts. The sun painted golden streaks across the grass, and there he stood, happily listening.

'That's a lovely voice you got there, Princess!' TCG's words floated towards her, carrying admiration in his voice.

He settled onto the soft and delicate grass. Liana sat up, startled by his sudden appearance. She glanced at him, her tear-streaked face a mix of vulnerability and defiance. 'I don't need compliments from you,' she sighed.

'I'm going to say whatever I want,' TCG replied, his smile widening, unable to hide his pity for her.

'Why do you care about me so much?' Liana questioned, turning away from him.

'Because it's my job to care,' TCG responded softly, his voice filled with an underlying tenderness that hinted at his deeper feelings.

'Why?' cried Liana, her emotions overwhelming her.

'You can't always say 'why'. Whatever happens in your life was meant to happen,' TCG sighed, his voice profoundly understanding, 'Someone once taught me that.'

'I hate it when you shout at me! Is that meant to happen as well?' she responded.

TCG winced, regret flashing across his eyes, 'Listen, I'm sorry. And I don't understand why it hurts you so much when I shout. People have gone through much more with me, and I don't think they've complained this much!' he laughed.

'So, what are you going to do now?' Liana asked, her eyes brimming with tears, seeking answers in TCG's gaze.

'What do you mean?' TCG replied, his expression curious.

But Liana's vulnerability burst forth, a storm breaking through the calm, 'Are people going to keep on trying to kidnap me?' Her words tore from her throat, raw and desperate. Hot tears streamed down her reddened cheeks.

TCG stood up, his gaze intense. 'Listen up, girl,' he said softly. 'People are only after you 'cause you have something special about yourself. Do you understand me? Blossom.'

'What could I possibly have that these jerks want from me so badly? My life's so messed up.'

TCG's smile was enigmatic, 'Ever looked at yourself in the mirror, ma princess? You'll find your answer right there!'

Liana peered into the pool's reflection, her tear-streaked face staring back at her. 'Smile!' laughed TCG. 'That's the secret.'

He walked away, leaning against a nearby tree, watching Liana's puzzled expression. She smiled at herself, but she was still feeling confused.

'Is this just a way to make me smile?' Liana's voice was gentle, like a delicate petal twirling in a soft breeze.

'No,' laughed TCG, walking up to her, 'I guess you can't catch me, you loser!' he challenged and suddenly started running.

Liana's determination flared, 'Did you just call me a...? You're in for it,' she said, getting up and sprinting after him.

TCG glanced over his shoulder. Seeing her gaining ground, he pushed himself to run faster, laughter bubbling up from the bottom of his throat. Liana sprinted through the dense garden. Her breaths came in ragged gasps, and the sun peeked through the leaves, creating a patchwork of light and long shadows on the garden floor. Her legs felt tired, and her heart pounded in her chest, but she refused to give up.

Always one step ahead, TCG had a mischievous glint in his eyes. He slowed down, allowing Liana to catch up. 'Didn't I tell you?' he teased with a grin on his face.

'You got that wrong. You're the loser!' Liana retorted, and without hesitation, she pushed TCG.

He stumbled, arms flailing, and landed in a nearby swimming pool. Liana couldn't suppress her laughter, 'I got you by surprise, didn't I?' she teased, heading towards the kitchen doors.

TCG swam towards the edge of the pool. 'That girl, man,' he laughed loudly, pulling himself out with water dripping off him.

But he didn't mind being caught off guard; perhaps there was more magic in Liana's smile than the eye could see.

Joseph, looking resplendent in his police uniform, strolled into the kitchen; his eyes fell on Liana, who was happily smiling.

'Liana, you seem very happy today,' he said.

'Yeah, I taught TCG a lesson!' replied Liana, glancing up at him. Just then, her phone erupted into a cacophony of rings. Liana's nervousness spiked as she answered, 'Hi,' she said tentatively.

'I thought I'd give you a ring to see how you're doing,' the voice on the other end said.

'I'm fine, how about you?' sighed Liana.

'Ever since you flew out to America,' the voice continued, 'I've been so happy. I'm so freakin' glad you're away.'

Liana looked up at Joseph, rolling her eyes as the woman on the other line slammed the phone down. 'Who in the world was that?' asked Joseph, wrinkling his eyebrows.

'My granny,' sighed Liana.

'She sounds like a witch!' he murmured, 'How in the world do you cope with a grandma like that?'

'She's a difficult person. That's why I flew to America for my studies, and now my life's gone upside down,' Liana said, slumping back into her chair.

Joseph furrowed his brow, deep in thought. 'Well,' he said, 'at least you've got a granny who keeps things interesting. Most grandmas just knit sweaters and bake cookies.'

Liana's mischievous grin widened, 'Mine?' she said, in a mysterious tone, 'She brews potions and hexes the neighbours.'

Joseph blinked, 'Wait, what?' he spat, 'Are we talking about the same granny who sends birthday cards with glitter bombs?' he said sarcastically.

'The very same,' Liana confirmed with a grin, 'She's got a wicked sense of humour. Last week, she hexed Mr Thompson's garden gnome to laugh like a devil at midnight.'

Joseph cracked up, 'Your granny is a legend!' he leaned forward, happily smiling, 'Forget knitting; she's out there whipping up potions and flinging spells like it's a friendly neighbourhood bake-off!'

Liana laughed; making up stories about magical hexes and potions were funny if only her grumpy granny knew! But then, she wondered if only her granny had been kind, offering warm hugs instead of being cranky all the time. 'Only if,' Liana whispered to herself, 'Only if my granny was nice to me.'

Joseph saw her face drop and quietly listened to her whispers. 'I wish my mum was here to hug me and fill my life with true love,' she sighed, wiping a tear away from her cheek. 'And only if my dad hadn't left me. At least he could have comforted me in these miserable, lonely times!'

Joseph rested his hand on her shoulder, 'Don't worry. You've got TCG to help you through your hectic life,' he smiled.

'What?' Liana's voice sliced through the air. 'That's even worse, I hate him from the bottom of my heart!' Her words carried venom, each syllable dripping with hatred.

Joseph's eyebrows shot up, caught off guard by her sudden shriek. Suddenly, Steven entered the kitchen with a stern frown.

'Why are you yelling again?' he sighed, folding his arms in disgust.

'Because I want TCG dead!' she shouted, standing up.

'What?' TCG's voice echoed from the hallway.

Joseph glanced at Steven. 'I can't believe she just said that in front of two police officers,' he muttered.

TCG stormed into the kitchen, eyes ablaze, 'What did you bloody say?' he thundered, glaring at Liana.

She turned to face him, her fury unyielding, 'What the hell, are you blimey deaf? I said I want you dead!'

Chapter Ten
Alley's not bright! Havin' a lovely night!

'I'm trying to save you from getting killed, and that's what you say to me!' TCG shouted back. Liana's heart raced as she waited for the inevitable confrontation, but instead of an imminent furious outburst, TCG glared at her for a moment. He turned away, striding out of the kitchen, fuming.

'Oh, you're in for it now,' Joseph sighed, his eyes wide. 'You should have never said that!'

Steven leaned against the counter, his expression a mix of frustration and concern, 'Why do you have such a problem with him? He's done so much for you. Think about it,' he sighed.

'Can you take me back to Britain?' Liana's voice cracked. She felt trapped in this foreign land, a vulnerable teenage girl in a dangerous world.

'We can't do that,' stated Steven.

'Why not? You're the police, and this is not my country, so bloody get me out of here, right now!' she said in a loud voice.

'You really think TCG's going to let us do that,' laughed Steven.

'What? He's not the king or something!' glared Liana.

Joseph looked at her amusingly, a sly grin on his face, 'You definitely don't know who TCG is,' he whispered, 'He's the man, the gangster. It's in his name, Triple Caste Gangster!' He glanced at Steven, who shot him a warning look.

'You better say sorry to him!' demanded Steven, glaring at Liana.

'I am never going to say that!' she yelled. 'He's the one who caused it on himself!' She stormed out of the kitchen, leaving both men staring at her in utter astonishment.

'She's so stubborn,' muttered Steven.

But Joseph shook his head, a knowing smile playing on his lips. 'You really can't blame her, can you?' he said, 'Look at how much she's gone through. She's just confused; that's all it is.'

After spending a considerable amount of time in her room, Liana opened her door quietly and peeped out. The hallway was dark and quiet. It had been a long time since Steven and Joseph had left; Liana wasn't even sure if anyone was in the house. She stepped out into the cold hallway and tiptoed down the stairs. Wandering into the living room, she found everything still and quiet.

She quietly tiptoed back out into the hallway, and then, at that moment, she heard a noise as if someone had put a glass down. She peered through the lounge door, which was slightly ajar, and realised it was TCG drinking some Coke from a glass cup.

She stood behind the door, heard TCG sigh and put his glass on a nearby table again. Liana held her breath as she put her hand on the handle. She slowly opened the door and looked inside the room. It was pretty dark; only a bit of light came out of a lamp in the far corner of the room.

TCG immediately looked up at her and then looked down at his phone. He reclined on a sofa with his legs stretched out, one leg crossed over the other, exuding a casual confidence that belied the danger lurking within him. The lamplight cast shadows across his face, and his fingers danced over the phone screen.

Liana sensed an ominous tension in the room, yet an inexplicable force compelled her towards the sofa. With a blend of anxiety and curiosity, she perched on the edge, and as their eyes met, the room fell into an eerie silence.

'TCG,' she whispered, her voice filled with a hint of fear.

'Don't talk to me! I'm fed up with your bloody behaviour!' yelled TCG, his voice filled with disdain.

Liana felt like someone had just slapped her across her face; her heart sank, feeling like an unwanted intruder in his presence, 'I didn't mean to say that I want you dead,' she explained.

'I said shut the heck up,' TCG replied coldly.

Their exchange intensified, a tempest of emotions swirling beneath their words. 'Shut up yourself!' Liana suddenly screamed. The air crackled with tension, each syllable like a sharp dagger, 'I really hate you!' she yelled.

'Really? And what you said before was out of order. Do you understand me?' smirked TCG, a hint of contempt seeping into his voice. Liana glared at him with her blue eyes.

'Get the hell out of my face!' shouted TCG.

'You get the hell out of my life!' yelled Liana, staring at him in frustration.

TCG stood up with defiance, 'Don't ever show your face in front of me, or I'll break it for you!' he yelled, his voice dripping with venom, as he stormed out of the room and slammed the door shut.

Liana's gaze fell upon the clock, its ticking mocking her. She realised that it was getting late. Curiosity washed over her, compelling her to whisper to herself, 'I wonder why you always go out at this time.' Driven by confusion, she reluctantly rose from the sofa and quietly opened the door, peering into the dimly lit hallway, her unease growing with each step she took.

She saw TCG opening the front door and disappearing into the darkness outside. Liana quickly stepped into her shoes and flung the front door open. The garden stretched out before her, but there was no sign of TCG. 'He really does walk fast, man!' she muttered to herself, stepping out of the garden and onto the pavement. Suddenly, she saw TCG disappearing around the corner, sparking a mixture of fascination and dread within her.

A chilly breeze blew around TCG, making him shiver; he walked in the shadows, shoving his hands in his pockets. As Liana trailed behind him, an ominous gust of wind blew, sending shivers down her spine, and the thrill of the chase mingled with a growing sense of unease. As she succumbed to the twisted allure that drew her deeper into the darkness, she saw TCG vanishing into a gloomy alley. Pausing, she looked into the alley, squinting her eyes. It was as if he had just disappeared into thin air. Curiously, she continued walking up the dark alley.

Her eyes caught sight of a figure standing in the shadows. It then stepped out and headed up the alley. Was it TCG?

A streetlamp shone at the end of the alley, and then she saw TCG stepping beneath the light, bathed in its spectral radiance. But someone trailed him, a shadow within shadows.

Liana looked suspiciously at the man following TCG. He had something firmly held in his hand. Her eyes widened with shock as she realised he had a metal spanner in his hand, its edges glinting malevolently.

The brutal desire for vengeance unfolded. A man charged from the alley's depths, slamming an object into TCG's face; blood sprayed, and TCG staggered. Then, the man who was following him smashed the spanner into the other side of his face, causing it to bleed profusely. He struck him again with immense force and power, causing TCG to fall to the ground. A third man emerged, clad in black clothes, his boot hovered, poised to crush TCG's skull.

TCG quickly rolled across the ground and painfully picked himself up. He leapt towards the man, smashing his knuckles into his jaw, followed by a brutal uppercut. The powerful impact sent the man flying into the cold wall behind him.

The man holding the spanner charged at him; TCG grabbed the man's arm aggressively, twisting it with brutal force. Bones cracked, and the alley echoed with painful screams, yet TCG wasn't done; his knee rocketed upwards, a flying strike to the man's nose, blood sprayed, and his world blurred. TCG struck him with a powerful flying sidekick straight into his neck, causing it to snap backwards.

The man stubbornly still tried to smash the spanner in TCG's head. TCG swiftly pulled his gun out and shot him at point-blank range in the face. Liana's frantic gaze swept the alley, seeking a way to help TCG; his shots echoed, each a desperate plea for revenge, 'Blimey, won't you guys just leave me alone!' shouted TCG. His voice, rough and defiant, reverberated off the walls.

He then skilfully struck the third man who was standing in front of him with a spinning back kick followed by a roundhouse straight into his nose. Liana was about to shout out to TCG as another man crept behind him, yanking TCG's head backwards.

Liana stared in bewilderment as she saw TCG yanking the man's arms off his neck; he turned to face the man and shot him in the side, causing him to collapse on the ground. She looked at TCG with amazement because the men who were fighting TCG had strength and power. But he had swiftly dodged them and took them on with huge stamina as if they were a joke to him.

Then, a man in white emerged, slowly walking up to TCG. His shades concealed eyes that had seen too much, and something lethal glinted in his hand. Liana's heart raced. 'TCG!' she screamed, but her voice vanished into thin air.

The man raised his hand, and a bullet suddenly materialised out of nowhere, slicing through the air with lethal speed. The bullet struck TCG in the side of his shoulder. He fell onto the ground in agony.

The man walked up to TCG, grabbed him by the shoulder, and yanked him up. He slammed TCG against the wall and hissed, 'Where's the girl? Don't be a hero and bloody tell me. Ya daft shithead.'

TCG's defiance flared, 'She's where she belongs!' he shouted.

The man slammed the gun into TCG's face, making him feel as if he was going to fall to the ground and die, 'You better tell me!' yelled the man, poking the barrel of the gun into TCG's head. He had him pressed against the cold alley wall.

'No!' yelled Liana, running and grabbing the spanner from the floor; it was the only weapon within reach.

The man turned, eyes narrowing; she swung the spanner, and it connected with flesh and bone.

Liana felt two hands grab her by the shoulders. She was flung to the ground; she looked up and saw a man standing above her, pointing his gun at her, 'What the hell are you doing, you moron? Put the gun down, Dave!' shouted the man who had the spanner bashed into his face, 'Have you gone mad?'

'No, Ned, I'm just warning her,' Dave muttered.

An SUV was parked over at the end of the alley. Liana saw Ned slam the gun into TCG's face again, making him black out. Dave yanked Liana up and shoved her into the vehicle's cold embrace.

Liana looked around worriedly as the door was slammed shut. The driver glanced back, a wolfish smile on his lips; he was a young man with secrets hiding in his eyes. 'Having a nice night, chick?' he smiled. Liana ignored his sarcastic remark, and then the opposite door to hers opened. Dave shoved TCG into the car and slammed the door shut with a loud thud.

Ned jumped in the front passenger seat and smirked, 'Finally, we got the bloody shithead. I told Dave to go with Ken, so he won't be coming with us.'

'Yeah, we need to get going quickly,' said the driver, 'And get onto Ken and tell him that he better not say a word to my dad that we've got the girl.'

'Why not?' yelled Ned. 'Your dad needs both of them. That's the main point of us bloody getting TCG,' he said, staring at the driver.

'Are you going to listen to me or not?' the driver's voice cracked like a whip.

'Yes, Boss, I'll get on to him then,' muttered Ned, immediately pulling his phone out.

Liana listened to the two men, hate and fear consuming her. She turned to look at TCG, whose eyes were shut. Blood seeped out of his shoulder, causing Liana's eyes to tear up. A thought struck her heart: *I wanted you dead, but who's going to protect me now?*

She clutched his hand tightly, 'Wake up!' she whispered.

Tears rolled slowly down her cheeks and fell upon his arm, 'Why are you not responding?' she cried.

Liana felt the driver and Ned go silent. She looked up and saw them staring back at her. 'What are you staring at?' Liana snapped. Tears continued to roll down her cheeks and onto TCG's arm. Ned smirked, but the driver silenced him with a glare.

The driver pulled away from the curb, and Liana nestled her head against TCG's shoulder, their fingers still entwined. After a long, nerve-racking period, she gently traced her finger over the long, deep scar on his hand, which travelled up his arm. With a gentle push, she lifted his sleeve to reveal more of the scar's journey. But then, her gaze shifted to something unexpected: black calligraphy inked onto his forearm. She followed the elegant letters, reading the sentence quietly, '*Naila, I promised you.*' Liana's eyes met TCG's closed ones, and she gently brushed her thumb against his cheek. 'Naila,' she whispered, her breath warm against his cheek, 'I wonder what promise you made to her.' As the SUV's engine sputtered to silence, she rolled his sleeve back down, lost in thoughts of the mysterious promise on his skin.

The driver stepped out of the vehicle and walked towards Liana's door. Swinging it open, he smiled at her. His smile was mocking, but she realised there was something deeper in it than anybody could imagine. He grabbed her trembling hand, gently pulling her out and leading her up a winding path.

In the murky embrace of darkness, her senses were rendered blind, yet the man's unyielding grip persisted as they approached the imposing twin doors. With a resounding creak, the doors swung open, revealing a breathtaking grandeur that stole Liana's very breath away. He made her walk up a crimson-carpeted staircase, the plush rug flowing like a river of blood beneath her feet, the marble floors whispered secrets as she climbed, and opulent chandeliers cast their luminous glow. This was no ordinary place. It was like a palace of secrets.

The man took her into a room adorned with vast glass windows decorating the walls; couches lined the walls, inviting yet cold.

Above her, a glass chandelier hung like a frozen tear. The man handcuffed her hands and walked out of the room with a grin which held hidden desires.

Liana sank to the marble floor, hands bound behind her back. Tears blurred her vision as she leaned on the cold wall, and within seconds, sleep descended, wrapping her in its velvet embrace.

Chapter Eleven
What shall she find? Freezin' your mind!

Liana's eyes shot open. The air was thick with tension, and sunlight streamed through the window, casting sharp lines across the floor. She blinked, disoriented, her mind racing to catch up with her surroundings.

She heard the noise of a door being opened. She looked around and saw the young man walking in, his eyes staring directly at her. Sunlight flooded the room, causing Liana to realise that she had been sleeping for a while. The room bore the scars of her captivity, hours, maybe days.

As he approached, the gleam of his jewellery captured Liana's gaze. His fingers, adorned with multiple rings, sparkled in the sunlight, each one a symbol of his power and wealth. The intricate designs of the rings showcased precious gemstones, which dazzled with every movement, reflecting the dangerous allure he emanated.

Around his neck hung an expensive gold chain, gleaming under the sun's rays. Its weight seemed to symbolise the burdens he carried physically and metaphorically. Liana couldn't help but wonder about the secrets it harboured, the shadowy history woven into its links.

She observed his approach with a mix of apprehension and curiosity. His movements were calculated, every step purposeful, as if he were navigating a dangerous walk. The way he toyed with the key, a small, harmless object, sent shivers down her spine. Was it a smile that curved his lips or a predator's snarl? The ambiguity unsettled her.

'I bet you're so confused,' he laughed and crouched beside her, 'My name's Lorenzo,' he whispered as if trying to share a secret.

Liana's gaze remained fixed on the floor, unwilling to meet his eyes. The handcuffs, once unyielding, surrendered to Lorenzo's will; their chilled metal links gave way to the gentle press of his fingers, and as they slipped off, the room seemed to breathe out a collective sigh of relief or perhaps a sense of anticipation.

Lorenzo remained crouched, his eyes never leaving Liana's face. Now free, Liana's wrists bore the imprint of the cuffs, a memory etched into her skin. But this wasn't just physical freedom; it was the release of something more profound, an unspoken pact between captor and captive.

Lorenzo's murmur sent shivers down her spine. 'Liana,' he breathed, the syllables laden with promise. His strong fingers traced the wall behind her as if he were writing out what was floating in her mind. 'Do you wish for anything?' he whispered with a smile.

Liana stood up sharply; her instincts screamed silence, but her mind raced. Why was he here? What did he want? And where was TCG, the shadow who haunted her?

'Where's TCG?' she demanded, voice sharp, eyes firm.

Lorenzo stepped back and laughed. 'I was afraid you would say that. He told me to send you a message before we let him free,' he smirked. Liana felt a shiver go down her spine as she heard the words, *'Let him free'*.

'What message?' she pressed.

'He said you hated him, and he wanted to tell you that he hates you and he wants you dead!' laughed Lorenzo.

Liana felt her heart shatter, and she burst out crying, not caring that he was looking at her.

'No one likes you, and no one cares about you. Liana, what have you done to yourself?' sighed Lorenzo.

Liana slid down the wall and hugged her knees, sobbing her heart out. Lorenzo's hand closed around hers, and he yanked her up. 'Look at me,' he commanded, his smirk both cruel and enticing.

Liana didn't look at him and carried on crying.

'I have killed many people, but I don't feel like killing you,' he smiled. 'Choices have consequences, Liana, and unexpected alliances.'

The room's door swung open, revealing a teenage girl. She glided in, her crimson dress trailing behind her like a river of blood. Her brown eyes bore into Lorenzo and Liana, making them feel a chilling intensity of evilness. Each step she took echoed on the marble floor, her heels tapping a sinister rhythm.

Her red lips were fixed into an evil smile, and her eyes were lined with thick black eyeliner, 'I see you've brought the big bloody bitch,' she taunted, closing the distance between herself and Liana.

Liana's gaze flickered towards the girl's hand; she was holding a terrifying-looking gun. 'I wish TCG were here to see your crying face,' she smirked. In one swift motion, she slammed the weapon into Liana's face, sending her flying across the floor, face forward. Lorenzo took a deep breath and let out a gasp in bewilderment.

'Oh, Lorenzo,' the girl purred, her voice like a smooth blade. 'I hope you don't have any pity for her. Do you understand me?' she smirked, turning towards him.

'Yes, Eulalia,' sighed Lorenzo. Eulalia laughed sharply and left the room with pride and arrogance.

Lorenzo looked at Liana. She lifted her head, and blood dripped down her lip, splattering onto the marble floor. 'Are you alright?' gasped Lorenzo, looking at her as if he could see a ghost.

But Liana was no damsel in distress; she abruptly stood up, fury igniting her veins. Her fist swung towards Lorenzo's face, a coordinated and calculated strike.

Lorenzo's smile widened, a glimmer of admiration in his eyes, 'Yeah, you've got skilful timing,' he acknowledged, deftly blocking Liana's punch with the precision of a seasoned fighter, 'But I think you forgot something. I'm a kickboxing expert,' he laughed mockingly. 'And yeah, you definitely got the same skill as your dad.'

'I don't have a freakin' dad!' yelled Liana. 'He left me, like everyone else has!'

'Oh, yes, how can I forget,' he said, passing her a tissue to dab her lip.

Lorenzo turned towards the window and stared into the abyss beyond. Liana seized her chance and sprinted towards the door, adrenaline propelling her forward.

Lorenzo's shout echoed after her as she yanked the door open and bolted into the unknown. 'No, you don't!'

Up a grand hallway, she raced, her heart pounding and her breathing heavy. She had no plan; desperation started kicking in, and Lorenzo's footsteps were closing in.

She quickly looked around, seeking escape, and there they were: long, gold-flowing curtains. She darted behind them, her heart hammering against her ribs.

Lorenzo thundered past the curtains and down the grand stairs. After a while, she popped her head out and looked around. Everything was clear and quiet. She descended a set of stairs, her steps silent like the calm morning breeze.

She ended up in a long and magnificent hallway. She hid behind a door as voices echoed up to her, 'He's downstairs in the basement, but Ken said that he had lost the girl,' said a man in an angry voice.

'What do you mean lost the girl?' another voice erupted, which sounded very familiar to Liana.

'If Lorenzo brought TCG into the house, then why didn't he bring Liana?' a quieter voice reasoned, 'I just don't understand?'

The familiar voice said calmly. 'Tell Ned and Dave to send their search parties out now.'

'Yes, boss.'

Liana felt her throat tighten as she heard their footsteps drifting off. She calmed her breathing and ran through the hallway. 'Where could the basement stairs be?' she muttered to herself.

Liana ran into a massive room with sliding doors in the far corner. The mansion seemed deserted as if its occupants had vanished into thin air. She tiptoed towards the sliding doors and slid them open.

Her gaze fell onto a beautiful kitchen. She brushed the gleaming countertops with her fingers; the glamorous units seemed very expensive. Suddenly, she saw something strange: a pristine white bannister leading downward. 'Stairs!' Her gasp echoed in the silence, shattering the stillness.

Suddenly, the banging of a door resonated in her ears, reverberating through the house. She ran with panic down the stairs and into a wide hallway. She felt lost and worried. *Where in the world was she?*

'What am I going to do?' sighed Liana, 'TCG's not even here,' she sobbed.

Thoughts collided like bricks hurling at her skull. Lorenzo had told her they had let TCG free, so who occupied the basement? Whose mansion was this? And did Lorenzo know her whereabouts through some hidden cameras?

Liana walked to the end of the hallway. Two paths diverged, left and right; she chose the left. There, she encountered yet another pair of stairs. 'Am I in some kind of maze?' she murmured, slowly walking down the stairs.

She glanced around in amazement as she stood on top of a balcony. Below the balcony, a metallic expanse of pipes and dangling cables greeted her. Her surroundings resembled a cold and utilitarian factory, but what else could she expect? This was the basement of a mansion.

Liana looked down. Stone pillars reached skyward like huge skyscrapers, and then she saw someone tied against one of the pillars. 'TCG!' Liana whispered, a mix of relief and fury.

She ran down the stairs, her heart thumping hard against her chest. TCG, bound and bloodied, stared at her with desperate eyes. The duct tape across his mouth stifled any sound, leaving him voiceless in the dimly lit basement.

Liana's smile faded as Lorenzo's ominous words resurfaced, 'He wants you dead!'

The thrill of seeing TCG suffering clashed with the gravity of the situation; she leaned forward, her voice low and taunting, 'It's lovely seeing you struggle!' she sniggered. 'Did it hurt when you got shot?' Her eyes locked onto TCG's annoyed face.

Liana leaned against the pillar. She ran her fingers through his long black hair and twisted a lock around her finger, causing him to sigh softly.

Liana let out a sharp laugh as she noticed his vulnerability. She whispered softly in his ear, 'Or does this hurt?' and pulled his hair, testing the limits of his endurance. TCG glared at her with his blazing eyes, which caused her to erupt with more laughter.

She walked behind the pillar and started untying the knots of the ropes that had prisoned TCG's hands. They were like ancient curses. Each loop was very tight, resisting her efforts. The ropes seemed to hold TCG in a tight grip, as did the weight of secrets and betrayal.

Liana spoke, her voice like a dangerous dagger. 'I just don't understand you,' she smirked, her warm breath brushing against TCG's ear. 'I know something is floating in your mind, making you freeze, right?' She suddenly laughed, a melody of menace. 'You hate me, don't you?' she said, moving on to the last knot.

Suddenly, Liana felt herself getting dragged down; someone had pinned her to the cold stone floor, and his grey eyes searched hers, 'Lorenzo, let me go!' she yelled.

Lorenzo stared at her and stuttered as if he was about to say something, then he took a deep breath, 'My dad is going to kill me.' His words hung in the air like poison.

He let Liana stand up, his fingers moving with practised urgency, undoing the last knot that bound TCG. Their gazes met, a silent exchange of fear and determination.

TCG pulled the duct tape off his mouth and looked at the balcony. Men were talking at the top of the stairs, their voices murmuring, a clandestine gathering of shadows.

Lorenzo's parting gift was chilling: 'Here, take this!' He handed TCG a gun and glanced back at Liana. His eyes held secrets, and he suddenly vanished into the labyrinthine aisles. 'Liana,' said TCG, looking at her with desperation.

Her smirk was annoying. 'Should I be listening to you?' she remarked, and then, with a mischievous smile spreading across her face, she stood by his side.

'We need to get out of here. Follow me,' he whispered. His voice was filled with urgency and panic. Liana followed him as he sprinted through the different aisles, where hundreds of pipes and wires hung from the walls.

A sudden shout erupted from nowhere, 'Bloody heck, how in the world did he escape?'

They heard the sound of running and men shouting, 'He's got to bloody be here, search the damn place!'

TCG caught sight of a skylight; he ran underneath it and glanced around. 'Here, Liana, climb this,' he said, lifting her onto a metal pipe. 'And make sure you push the skylight open!' he demanded, panic in his voice.

But danger was relentless. 'Over there!' yelled a man. Liana continued climbing up the pipe, holding the bolts firmly so she wouldn't slip. 'Stop her!' screamed a man, fury raging in his voice. 'How did she end up here?'

Liana looked towards the man and gasped, 'Fang!'

'There he is, Trever. Get him!' shouted one man to another who was running up to TCG.

'TCG, you thought it would be that easy escaping?' laughed Trever, arrogantly walking towards him.

TCG tried to fight him off but felt too weak to put all his power into action, 'Get the girl, Jet, before she gets away!' Trever's order was a battle cry. Fully agile as a panther, Jet lunged for Liana and grabbed her leg.

'Get off me, you jerk!' shrieked Liana. TCG looked up at Jet with anger and gave an uppercut in Trever's face, followed by a brutal roundhouse, causing him to fall to the ground.

Trever managed to stumble up quickly and threw a heavy fist towards TCG's nose, but he swiftly blocked it and twisted Trever's arm behind his back. With fury stabbing TCG's heart, he struck him in the neck with a powerful front snap kick. Trever let out a painful shriek, kicked TCG in the shin, and punched him in the face with full force. He then grabbed TCG's head and slammed it into the unforgiving stone wall.

'My name's not 'Jerk', it's 'Jet'!' Jet yelled sarcastically. His grip tightened around her waist, and he dragged her down. As she fell into his grasp, her eyes met TCG's.

TCG looked up at her, adrenaline surging through his veins. Suddenly, he got the strength to push Trever away from him. He gave a powerful hook in his face, causing his nose to bleed, and then, with skilful timing, he gave a flying knee strike into his chest, causing him to fall backwards. TCG grabbed Trever's head and continuously smashed it into the brick wall.

Lorenzo's precious gift, a concealed gun, was his last resort; he drew it swiftly out of his pocket and shot Trever a good few times all over the body; the shots echoed throughout the mansion.

Jet looked down at TCG from the top of the pipe with fear and astonishment, 'How the hell do you have a gun?' he shouted, quickly pulling his own gun out. TCG shot a bullet with calculated precision, trying not to get Liana accidentally. She shrieked as Jet and TCG continued to shoot bullets at each other. A bullet skimmed TCG's arm, making him bleed. Ignoring the blood and searing pain, he climbed the pipe with blood oozing from his wounded arm.

Jet's leg became his lifeline, 'Get the heck off me!' shouted Jet, trying to kick TCG in the face. Sweat trickled down TCG's eyebrow as he tried to drag him down with full force.

'Come on, you idiot, shoot him!' shouted Fang from the bannister. Jet pointed his gun down towards TCG and was about to pull the trigger when TCG suddenly yanked the gun out of his hand and shot him in the side. Jet yelled out of agony and unbearable pain.

TCG gave a powerful punch to his side and flung him off the pipe, causing him to land on the floor, face forward.

'Come on, Liana, get a move on!' shouted TCG; his urgency propelled her up the pipe quicker than ever. She eventually pushed open the skylight, gasping for fresh air.

'You just watch. I'm going to get you and gun you down. Ya asshole!' shouted Fang. TCG looked back at him and viciously swore at him.

Fang's phone emerged from his pocket, and frantic calls summoned reinforcements. 'They're going to be in the garden. Get them!' he yelled, sweat trickling down from his forehead.

TCG and Liana clawed their way onto the grass outside. Liana whispered, 'What are we going to do now?'

'Follow me,' TCG replied, sprinting across the vast, eye-catching patio that seemed to sink them into its extraordinary beauty. It had raised flower beds bursting with colour, and vibrant Daises, Roses, and Marigolds danced in the soft wind, creating a meadow-like atmosphere.

A beautiful fountain adorned the patio. Its trickling water danced in the warm air, resembling an oasis-like ambience. The soft grass looked like velvet carpet; its vibrant green hue invited bare feet to sink into its softness. The early morning dew danced on each blade of grass, each droplet catching the rays of the sunlight, creating a magical sparkle that looked like a canvas for natures artistry.

Suddenly, a Merc drove in front of TCG and sharply braked, nearly ramming him over, 'This way!' shouted TCG, turning his head backwards to ensure Liana followed him.

A pursuer leapt from the Merc and started chasing them, 'Blimey, can it get any worse?' yelled TCG, sprinting towards the huge imposing gates.

Liana's panic was obvious. Her voice was urgent, 'What are we supposed to do?' she cried out. TCG spun around, adrenaline surging as he assessed their dire situation. An angry man was closing in, fuelled by determination, and the gate loomed ahead, a formidable barrier between them and freedom.

'We've got to climb it!' exclaimed TCG. He seized the metal bars like a seasoned climber and started climbing up the gate with immense speed and power.

Liana looked up at him in horror, and TCG's frustration spilt over. Time was slipping away, and the man's footsteps grew louder. 'Why are you not climbing? You dope!' shouted TCG.

'I don't know how to flipping climb a gate that's triple the size of me,' cried Liana. She saw the man running up to her and attempted to scramble up the gate, desperate to follow TCG's lead, but her hands slipped, and her feet found no foothold.

TCG looked down at her in anger and disappointment. The man yanked Liana away from the gate and tightened his grasp on her shoulders, 'Now, Mr Squirrel, it's time for you to jump down,' he smirked, looking up at TCG.

TCG glared at the man, 'Sure, it will be a pleasure, ya bastard,' he replied, his voice a chilling whisper. In one swift motion, he leapt down and drew his gun. The deafening shot echoed through the air, and crimson droplets splattered the ground; the man crumpled, releasing Liana from his grasp. She staggered back, her fear now mingled with a strange sense of horror.

TCG flung Liana's arms over his neck as if she weighed no more than a feather. The rough texture of the gate's metal dug deep into his palms as he began to climb. Liana, her heart racing, clung to him with desperation. Her fingers dug into the fabric of his shirt, and she pressed her cheek against his shoulder with fear.

'Oi!' screamed a man, his voice thundering off the nearby buildings. His footsteps thundered on the ground as he ran up to them.

'Hold on!' TCG shouted to Liana. He reached the top of the gate, his fingers grazing the edge. With a swift motion, he swung Liana in front of him, lifting her effortlessly. She clung to him, her legs dangling over the other side. She shrieked like a little girl as he released her. She felt herself falling and then hitting the ground with brutal impact that sent pain screaming throughout her body.

'You can now open your eyes,' teased TCG, crouching beside her. 'We're on the ground!' His laughter mingled with the wind, but Liana couldn't bring herself to look; fear had frozen her, and her body hurt so much.

The man grabbed the other side of the gate as if he were a prisoner behind bars, 'Hey, bulldog, enjoy yourself in your dog kennel,' smirked TCG, and without hesitation, he drew his weapon and shot the man straight in the head, causing him to collapse on the ground with blood streaming down his forehead.

'Come on, let's go!' TCG shouted as he started running. Liana sprinted after him, her determination propelling her forward. The relentless sun bore down, scorching her skin. Thoughts raced through her mind, but her physical pain slowed her down. The world seemed to sway, and her vision blurred at the edges.

The hot sun shone into her eyes, turning the world into a hazy mirage. She squinted, her vision narrowing. The sky shimmered, and the asphalt seemed to waver under her feet. Her throat tightened, parched and raw. It was like an invisible hand had clenched around her windpipe, stealing her precious oxygen.

And then it hit her, a sudden impact like someone had slammed a brick into her skull; pain radiated from the back of her head, and she staggered. 'TCG!' she cried, sobbing intensely. Desperation overwhelmed her, and TCG, who was at the far end of the street, pivoted sharply to find Liana rooted in place, her fingers clutching her throat and tears streaming down her face.

Trembling, she extended her hand towards him, her voice choked with desperation. 'TCG, I can't do this.'

Her legs gave way, and she collapsed onto the hard pavement, her blonde hair fanned out around her, a fragile halo against the harsh reality, the ground pressed against her cheek, cool and unyielding.

TCG's footsteps thundered like a desperate plea as he sprinted back to Liana. He knelt near her, panic spreading across his face.

'Get up!' he whispered, his voice intense, but Liana lay motionless, her breaths shallow, her gaze distant.

'Why does everyone hate me?' Her words were a broken whisper. 'Why does everyone want me dead? Why has everyone left me? WHY?' The anguish tore through her, leaving her vulnerable and exposed, like a fragile thread unravelling in the storm.

TCG's resolve solidified; he cradled her fragile form, his thumb gently wiping away the tears that clung to her cheeks. 'I will never leave you,' he vowed softly as her eyes slowly shut, surrendering to unconsciousness.

Chapter Twelve
Spittin' the bad swear! Got the touch you can't bear!

The wind blew softly through TCG's hair. His lips remained firmly set in a straight line, and his jet-black eyes gazed at the surroundings, absorbing every detail. 'Where shall we head then?' Steven asked, his voice cutting through the wind as he sped through the busy traffic on his blue and red Kawasaki.

'Don't drop me off in my third house because I think Fang knows that address,' sighed TCG, flicking his hair from his face.

'Shall we go to your first house then?' Steven suggested.

'Yes, that would be a good choice,' said TCG, looking around rapidly with his sharp eyes.

'They took both of you quite far away, didn't they? We're still in Baltimore!' Steven said in astonishment. 'How's Liana's breathing, now?' he inquired, adjusting his motorbike helmet.

'Well, she's better,' sighed TCG, glancing down at Liana. Silence settled over them for a while. TCG nudged Liana and whispered, 'Liana, get up!' But she remained still and unresponsive. 'Liana, come on, get up!' he urged, gently shaking her arm.

Liana's eyes slowly opened, adjusting to the sun's warm embrace. 'Woah, careful!' TCG's voice carried a hint of amusement. 'You'll fall off the motorbike!' he warned her.

His presence behind her was solid and protective. His arms encircled her waist, securing her to the speeding machine.

Liana sat up straight, brushing TCG's hands aside. He quickly withdrew them. The sunlight painted his features that held secrets and danger. At that moment, she wondered if she was running towards freedom or deeper into TCG's wild games.

'Liana, you're up,' laughed Steven, glancing backwards. Some of his words drifted into the wind.

After a lengthy and tiring drive, they finally reached their destination. 'Come on, Liana! We need to get inside!' sighed TCG. Steven took his helmet off and smiled at Liana, who appeared as though she'd just stepped off a turbulent plane ride.

After walking inside, Liana made herself comfortable on the sofa in the living room. 'I bet you're glad to be home!' teased Steven, glancing at TCG's battle-worn face. He settled next to TCG, concern showing in his features. 'Now let me clean your wound and bandage you up,' he sighed. 'Your arm has taken more hits than a punching bag. How are you still standing?' His smile softened the gravity of the situation.

'I'm a tough gangster! What do you expect?' laughed TCG.

Liana lay on the sofa and stared at the ceiling. Steven, watching her from the opposite couch, said, 'You seem lost in thoughts!' he chuckled.

'You keep your stupid self out of my thoughts. You daft officer,' Liana snapped, her voice filled with frustration.

After getting his arm bandaged, TCG stood up from his seat and sat beside her. He grabbed her hand gently and stared at the ceiling.

'Who is Lorenzo, and why did he help us?' asked Liana.

'Lorenzo is Fang's son,' TCG began. 'The reason why he helped us remains a mystery, but I think the reason might be... because he probably felt sorry for your baby face, and he didn't want you to get harmed!' teased TCG. 'And that's why he didn't tell his dad about you. These guys, man. They've got their own agendas nowadays!' he smirked.

'Shut it,' Liana retorted, her irritation genuine. 'And I don't have a baby face!' she yelled. 'Lorenzo told me that you hate me, and you want me dead? Is this true, or did he lie?' she asked.

'Yes, he definitely lied. He just wanted to divert your mind because girls fall for what guys say, especially stupid girls like you!' teased TCG again.

'I don't fall for any of the rubbish that guys say!' spat Liana. 'Anyway, how did Steven find us?' she said, glancing at Steven.

Steven chuckled and said. 'Luckily for you two, I happened to be on patrol. I saw TCG walking with you in his arms; I nearly had a heart attack. I thought something really bad had happened to you!' he laughed in relief.

But Liana couldn't resist one last question. 'Why was Black Hawk's daughter in Fang's house? You know, the girl with a peculiar name... Eulalia!' she asked curiously.

TCG ran his fingers through his hair, weariness engraved into his expression. 'Well, we suspect that Fang's party and Black Hawk's party have joined forces to take us down.'

Liana sat up and looked into TCG's eyes. 'Why the heck do they have a problem with me? What have I done to them?' she said in a cocky tone, her voice dripping with defiance.

TCG and Steven exchanged glances, their silence amplifying the charged atmosphere. TCG's relaxed shrug only fuelled Liana's fire. 'I don't know, maybe because you're a special girl,' he laughed. 'And like I said before, the answer lies in your gorgeous smile.'

'Shut up!' yelled Liana, standing up and walking towards a table.

'You know I really hate it when you tell me to shut up!' said TCG, glaring at her.

Liana leaned against the table, her smirk slicing through the tension. 'Why? Can't you handle it that someone can finally shatter your pride?'

TCG rose from the sofa, closing the distance between himself and her. His voice dropped to a dangerous whisper. 'Say that one more time,' he said in a low, threatening tone.

Liana's fiery gaze bore into his eyes, and she repeated the rude sentence. 'Can't you handle it that someone can finally shatter your pride?' she yelled; her harsh words had barely left her mouth when a stinging, brutal slap collided with her cheek. It sent shockwaves through her entire body. Pain flared across her skin, and her vision blurred momentarily. Anger and shock struck Liana's vulnerable heart. With trembling fingers, her hand instinctively rose to her reddened cheek. Her eyes, aflame with rage, bore into TCG's, and she blurted out a vicious swear, the syllables sharp and venomous, cut through the charged air like shards of broken glass.

Steven gasped. 'How can you utter such a bad word like that? Where does your brain go at such a young age?'

The swear that Liana had just uttered made TCG feel like she had just slapped him fifty times over in the face. 'I wish I'd never flippin' met ya!' he bellowed. 'Get the heck out of my house, you dumb bitch!'

'It's good I came into your bloody life and shattered your pride, you daft bastard!' she yelled, bursting into tears. She stormed out of the room and slammed the door shut behind her.

'You're actually going to let her walk outside all alone?' shouted Steven.

'Yeah, let her find out what reality is all about!' TCG yelled.

'I can't believe you!' yelled back Steven.

'Did you hear what she just said to me? I've never in my life sworn like that. Such disgusting words have never even crossed my mind, and you expect me not to be burning with anger. You should be glad I didn't bloody break her!' spat TCG, staring at Steven.

'I know she's really rude, but you're the one who triggered her off. Please don't let her run off again,' sighed Steven.

TCG glanced at Steven's face, then at the living room door. He took a deep breath and then, without hesitation, bolted out of the room.

'Liana!' TCG screamed as he ran out of the front door, chasing after her. She glanced back, her pace quickening, and she swung the garden gates open. 'Liana, come back!' he yelled, desperation in his voice.

'Stay away from me! Don't even think of coming close to me!' Liana yelled back.

TCG took a deep breath, and then, like a bullet train, he picked his speed up, catching up to her within seconds. 'Stop being so stubborn!' he shouted, grabbing her by her arm.

'Why shall I stop being stubborn?' she cried, struggling to get free.

TCG gently placed his hands on her shoulders and gazed into her ocean-blue eyes. His voice softened, holding a trace of love and care. 'Secrets have turned into dark secrets!' he murmured.

Her teary eyes were mixed with fear and anger. 'Why do you keep trying to show me that you care for me and love me? Can't you leave me alone?' she cried. 'And stop touching me!' She pushed TCG's hands off her shoulders, her breaths coming in ragged gasps.

'Come on, Liana!' TCG smiled, holding her hand. 'Let's go inside.' As they entered the front garden, Liana tried to free herself from TCG's tight grasp. But his grip remained firm.

'Let go! I'm not a bloody one-year-old learning to walk!' Liana's voice was mad with frustration as she yanked her hand away from him. TCG sighed, locking eyes with her teary gaze; she took a few steps back, her eyes never leaving his face. Then, unexpectedly, he reached for her arm, pulling her towards himself. His touch was gentle and possessive as his hand tightly gripped her shoulder. 'Liana,' he whispered, his breath warm against her ear. 'I don't know how to express how much I want you to stay safe,' he said, releasing her and heading towards the front door. 'And I'm not sure if you'll ever truly understand just how much I care for you.'

Liana stood there, astonished by his confession, before slowly following him inside.

In the lounge, TCG stood with a hint of mockery in his laughter. 'Liana, I just want to repeat that you're a stupid young chick with a big nasty gob, and yeah, defo, you've got a big attitude problem!'

Liana leaned against the far wall. 'You're the one that can't keep your big gob shut!' she yelled.

Steven, caught in the crossfire, attempted to calm the heated situation. 'Liana, I think you should speak with some manners,' he smiled, turning his face towards her.

'You keep your assumptions to your stupid self, you asshole,' she smirked.

Steven's expression shifted from surprise to bewilderment. 'Did you just call me an asshole?' he asked in disbelief.

'Yes, Officer Steven, I called you an asshole,' she replied calmly.

'See, just look at her attitude!' TCG said mockingly.

Liana's glare intensified, 'You should keep your hands under control!' she snapped. 'I should handcuff your hands, then we'll see what you'll do.'

'Then I'll kick the living daylights out of you,' spat TCG.

Liana looked at him, her defiance unwavering as she stood straight. Steven watched, jaw-dropping, as she launched herself into an aerial manoeuvre at lightning speed, her legs made a perfect split in mid-air. Her foot struck TCG's stomach, propelling him backward. He crashed into the chairs and landed awkwardly on his hands. Steven's eyes nearly fell out as he saw Liana eloquently land on her feet with her blonde hair cascading over her shoulders. TCG blinked; he really didn't know what hit him. Liana walked up to him and smiled. 'Don't underestimate me; you don't know what type of girl I am.'

TCG stared into her blue eyes and didn't know what to say. Steven erupted with laughter. 'Did you just fly in the air? I mean, you executed a perfect split in mid-flight!' Liana continued to stare at TCG, her expression unyielding.

'The best part was when I saw TCG flying backwards!' came a sudden voice. Everyone looked at the lounge door where Joseph was standing with a huge grin on his face. 'Now that was an awesome aerial. Girl, keep up the good work.'

'Shut up, Joseph!' TCG snapped, rising to his feet. He marched towards Liana, ready to slap her again.

'Keep your hands to yourself, or I'll kick you again,' Liana smirked. 'And I think you know where I'm going to kick you next!' she laughed, barging out of the room.

Joseph erupted with laughter, and Steven struggled to suppress his own laughter. 'That was not funny!' TCG protested, but Steven's laughter only intensified, joined by Joseph's encouragement.

'She's got guts, man, I wonder who she gets that from!' laughed Steven.

Still recovering from his amusement, Joseph choked out. 'I can't wait to see the moment when she kicks you again. And you clearly know where she's going to kick you!'

TCG, his pride wounded, hissed. 'Okay, now that's enough!' he sat on the couch, feeling embarrassed with himself.

Joseph grinned mischievously. 'Bro, I'm going to remember this day all my life. The cool dude got flung backwards by a girl. Did you just hear me? By a girl!' he teased. TCG glanced at Joseph and glared at him. Joseph's laughter bubbled up again, 'Take a chill pill, gangster!'

Chapter Thirteen
She's on bloody fire! Zak Ezra, you're a liar!

Liana kicked her feet against the chair, a rhythm of frustration. Joseph and Steven joked amongst themselves, sitting away from her, their laughter thundering through the room like a stormy day. She watched and listened to their harmonious jokes like an outsider. 'Anyway,' Joseph leaned back in his chair. 'It's nice being with you guys. And Liana, I certainly love your aerial!' He repeated, smiling and glancing at her.

'Yeah, I've got to say, Liana, you've got skill,' added Steven, trying to cheer her up.

Joseph stood up, shaking Steven's hand. 'I need to go back to the head office. See you sometime soon,' he stated. 'And you too, Liana,' he smiled. 'Where's TCG? Let me meet the guy, then I'll get going,' he said, climbing up the stairs.

Liana got up and walked solemnly to the kitchen. TCG came running down with Joseph, and their happy laughter filled the air. 'It's been good to have you here!' remarked TCG, patting Joseph's back.

'Yeah, bro, if you need any help, give me a bell, and I'll come running,' Joseph grinned back.

'Sure,' sighed TCG, opening the front door for him. He waved at him and walked into the living room, where Steven was fiddling around on his phone. Eventually, Liana walked in with a smile.

'You're smiling today!' chuckled TCG upon seeing her smile. 'How are you feeling?' His question hung in the air, and Liana's smile wavered.

'Great, until I saw you,' she replied, sitting on a sofa and opening a book. Steven lifted his gaze from his phone and looked at TCG's annoyed face.

'I just don't know what to say. You're so rude!' shouted TCG, his mood suddenly shifting.

'Why do you want me to be happy? Can't you just leave me to be who I want to be?' she yelled.

'Because your life's so mashed up,' TCG blurted. 'I thought I...'

'You thought you could fix it!' Liana's shout cut through the room. 'Shut up, I don't want to know you, you're no one to me!' she said, eyes aflame. TCG marched up to her in anger. 'Why does everyone think you've got something to do with me?' she shouted out.

He paused and stared into her burning eyes. The silence hung heavy. Steven stepped forward and spoke softly to her. 'Get going to your room, girl.'

Liana got up and barged off. The air clung to her like a shroud, heavy with secrets. She suddenly stopped and screamed, 'It's not my room. It's just another stupid room!'

Liana slammed her door shut and sank into the chair. She started thinking about Blood Beauty, the horrible guide who led her to Fang's lair, the winding path, the scent of damp earth, the whispered promises of power, and then Black Hawk's lair, a place of danger and hidden agendas. But it was the teenage girl, the one who wept over her father's (Black Hawk's) lifeless form, that haunted Liana. That girl had a father, a connection severed by death. Liana's heart sank. Why did her own father abandon her?

'Why?' Liana muttered to herself. 'Did they call Black Hawk's daughter Eulalia? Such a bloody weird name.' The name tasted bitter, like iron on her tongue.

Liana could hear TCG and Steven walking out of the house and locking the door behind them. She placed her hand on her head, tears streaming and emotions playing around with her heart.

After a while, she thought she'd walk around the house and exercise her legs. She wandered through the grand hallway, each step emphasising her isolation.

Eventually, she reached a bedroom door that loomed over her. Was it an invitation or a trap?

She stared at it for a while and then decided to walk off, but the door seemed to pull her in. She edged towards it and tried the handle; it swung open, and Liana found herself walking inside it.

The room stretched before her, an abyss of emptiness. Inside it, there was only a bed, a drawer, and a desk. It felt as if the glass windows held the room's secrets. Their panes, warped by the relentless passage of time, whispered stories of love, loss, and longing. They framed a view of the outside world, a world that had moved on, leaving this room frozen in its own quiet universe.

Liana's footsteps were quiet as she slowly crossed the cold marble floor. Her eyes were drawn towards a frame perched on the drawer's edge; a serene river flowed within it, with the moon's reflection dazzling in the water.

Curiosity tugged at Liana, so she pulled open one of the drawer compartments. To her surprise, it revealed an unexpected sight: guns of varying sizes lay in neat rows, their cold metal promising both protection and destruction. Liana smirked, recognising the signature of the enigmatic TCG, the man who connected the line between law and lawlessness.

'That's typical TCG for you!' she muttered; she was just about to shut the compartment when she saw a piece of paper ripped up in four. Grabbing it, she pieced it together, edges aligning like fractured memories. The image emerged: a woman cradling a newborn with TCG beside her, his gangster's grin softened by fatherly pride.

Liana gasped. 'So, you did have a family!' She shoved the pieces back into the drawer. 'I wonder what happened to your family?' she muttered. She walked over to the window and leaned on the ledge to look out, but as she did so, her hand crunched against something soft, a forgotten envelope. Dust clung to its surface, a testament to neglect.

With care, Liana blew away the thick layer of dust, revealing a letter within; its inked words danced across the page, hurriedly written and informal.

She carefully read each line, the weight of its contents sinking into her brain. She realised the room held more than furniture; it cradled secrets, regrets, and a past waiting to be unstitched.

And so, Liana continued to examine the ink-stained narrative, tracing the contours of a life hidden behind closed doors. Once skeletal and quiet, the room now pulsed with stories of love, loss, and the ache of unspoken truths.

Dear Naila

I'm scribblin' this in a real hurry. My trembling hand is smudging the ink as I try to write words on this freakin' bloody paper, I don't know if this letter's ever gonna find its way to you, but I've gotta give it a shot, ya know?

The air's thick with flipping tension, and every bleeding heartbeat feels like a ticking time bomb. I might not make it, ya feel me?

The shadows close in, and I fight them off, each breath a struggle, each step a desperate plea for survival, but damn, it's hard. The weight of our love and memories are pressing against my chest like a ton of bricks.

I ache for you, our baby, the fragile thread that binds us together.

And the most important thing I wanted to tell you is to take the baby to your sister's house. It will be much safer there.

Trust no one, not even your kin. The world is treacherous, and danger lurks in every shadow.

They're after you, the baby, and me!

From your caring husband
Zak Ezra

'What are you doing in my room?' TCG's voice sliced through the air, and Liana jumped, her heart pounding. His anger crackled like electricity, and before she could react, he snatched the letter from her hand, tearing it in front of her face. Liana's eyes widened, 'I didn't know you had a wife!' she blurted out, staring into TCG's mad eyes. He stood frozen, the paper remnants fluttering around him like confetti. 'Why don't you talk about her?' her voice rose, fuelled by frustration and curiosity. The room seemed to shrink, its walls closing in on his hidden secrets.

'Shut up!' TCG's shout echoed off the walls. 'Don't ever talk to me again. Get out of my room!' he shouted, sitting on his bed. She remained standing in her place. 'I said get out of my room, right now!' he yelled. She barged out of the room without saying another word, slamming the door behind her and leaving TCG alone. Anger swept through his brain, and fire burned in his chest. He felt hot and bothered, trapped in a hurricane of emotions.

He got up and strode angrily out of his room. As he walked down the stairs, he saw Liana lying on the sofa, flicking through her phone. She saw him coming down and started smirking at him.

TCG moved with deliberate grace, and each step was measured as if he were navigating a delicate walk. The room seemed to hold its breath, the air thick with anticipation. TCG approached the sofa, its plush cushions inviting comfort. He sat on the edge, with his gaze fixed on Liana, his eyes, pools of mystery and suspense, softened as they met hers, and at that moment, time stood still.

'What pain was the captain talking about before you shot him?' Liana's voice was softer this time, a plea to understand everything. Silence hung heavy, and TCG's gaze turned away from her. A storm brewing within him could be sensed.

Quietness filled the air. Liana's gaze rested on TCG; she realised he was getting heated up again. She sat up, edging closer, and held his hand. Her touch was gentle, fingers intertwining with his, but TCG, ever elusive, withdrew his hand as if it were a fragile secret he couldn't share. His eyes, once angry, now held a distant sadness; the room seemed to echo with the weight of unspoken words. Liana's heart sank; she wondered what haunted him, what made his heart burn up so much.

'The letter you read was the last letter that I sent to my wife,' he said, his voice holding sorrow and grief. 'When I was younger, Black Hawk's brother committed an evil crime. I was called by Sergeant Andrew to take him down, and I succeeded by catching up to him and killing him.' He let out a heavy sigh and paused. Liana gazed at him, patiently waiting for the rest of the story to be told; TCG looked at the ceiling and continued. 'Black Hawk wanted revenge and plotted against me. He planned to kill my family, and he did; he killed my wife just after I had sent the letter to her.'

Liana gasped, her hand flying to her mouth. A tear slipped down TCG's cheek, and for the first time, she saw vulnerability in the gangster's eyes. He quickly wiped the tear and slumped back onto the sofa.

'You mentioned a baby in your letter,' Liana said slowly.

She looked at him, realising that he wasn't paying attention to what she was saying. He appeared paralysed, gazing into her eyes with a gentle intensity that defied the sadness surrounding them.

TCG felt his heart racing against time. It suddenly skipped a beat with overwhelming affection. In that emotional moment, he reached for her, gently holding her hands and drawing her near. Gazing deeply into her bewildered blue eyes, he brought his face close to her ear, his touch conveying both comfort and closeness.

With a voice as gentle as the soft breeze, he whispered his emotions, letting his words speak volumes of his love.

'Liana,' he whispered, and at that moment, the room seemed to hold its breath as if waiting for her response.

Liana hesitated, her heart repeating his name, and then, with a tremor in her voice, she whispered back, 'Do you want to tell me something?'

TCG embraced her and whispered, 'The baby is you. You're my daughter!' his words hung in the air, a chilling revelation that shattered Liana's reality. She yanked her hands out of his grip, her heart thumping hard against her chest.

'I'm not your daughter!' she yelled, defiance and fear running within her.

'Liana, you're my daughter,' TCG persisted with desperation in his eyes. 'That's why I have sacrificed so much to protect you. I love you!' His words were a sinister promise, unravelling the fragile threads of her existence.

But Liana wasn't about to accept this twisted truth. 'I'm not going to listen to a liar!' she shouted, tears blurring the room.

'Liana, I'm not a liar,' TCG said softly, 'You're my daughter, and I promised Naila I'll do anything to keep you safe.'

'Shut the bloody hell up, you asshole!' yelled Liana, suddenly standing up. 'You're not my dad. You're a flipping jerk.' She fled, her footsteps pounding on the stairs, each step distancing her from the man who claimed her as kin.

Upstairs, she collapsed onto her bed, the mattress absorbing her tears. 'So, I did mean something to TCG!' she whispered. The room seemed to close in, its walls suffocating her; she pulled the blanket over her face, seeking refuge from a reality that no longer made sense.

The gangster's confession danced in her mind, a chilling melody of betrayal and secrets, and as she wept, she wondered what other horrors lay hidden in the shadows of her past.

A rapid knock on the door shattered the fragile cocoon of Liana's thoughts. She didn't answer; her tears were a silent testament to her pain. 'Liana,' came a whisper, insistent yet gentle. Still, she remained motionless, and her breathing quickened.

Then, the blanket covering her face was slowly pulled away. 'Sweetheart!' whispered TCG, standing above her with a soft smile.

'What kind of flipping father are you? You bloody dumped me,' she sobbed, tears trickling down her cheeks. 'Go away from me. I don't want to ever see you!'

'A father doesn't move away from his daughter, who is hurt and in pain,' he said, settling on the edge of the bed; his presence was both comforting and unsettling. Liana stayed silent, her heart a swirl of emotions.

Finally, she spoke, her voice like a fragile thread. 'A daughter doesn't refuse the help of her dad!'

Chapter Fourteen
Blood and Burning flames! Stabbin' is a deathly game!

'Your mum gave me this,' TCG whispered, his voice like a gentle breeze. 'She told me to give it to you.' He extended his hand, revealing a sky-blue coloured box. Its edges had softened over time; a white ribbon encircled it, delicate and unyielding, as if binding memories and secrets together. He passed it to Liana with a smile, 'It belonged to her,' TCG continued, his smile fragile yet full of tenderness, 'it's the only thing I've got of hers.' His gaze lingered on Liana as if seeking solace in her presence.

She slowly opened it, revealing a delicate and beautiful silver necklace. The chain seemed to hold the very essence of love, each link a testament to devotion. She traced her fingers along the chain, feeling the cool metal against her skin. At its centre hung a blue diamond pendant shaped like a heart. The gemstone was beautiful and eye-catching. The colour blue was deep and mysterious, like the sky in the summer days. She wondered how somebody had cut and polished the heart pendant so professionally.

As she fastened the necklace around her neck, the clasp smoothly clicking into place, she felt a sense of connection, an invisible thread linking her to her lost past. She closed her eyes, imagining her mother, a strong and beautiful woman who had endured pain and sacrificed so much for love, a love that no one could destroy.

The necklace now rested against her collarbone. She imagined her mother, who had worn it before her and bore so much pain just for her. She smiled at TCG for a second, and then it suddenly disappeared. 'Why did it take such a long time to tell me I am your daughter?'

TCG's expression softened as he spoke, his voice a gentle murmur. 'Because after your mum was killed,' he began. 'I thought it would be better for you if I stayed far away from you.' His eyes bore into Liana's, a silent apology etched in their depths. 'And I was definitely right because now that you're with me, the world is after you.'

TCG held Liana's hand and smiled. 'I remember when you were sitting on the bench. I didn't recognise you at first, but when I came to save you from that terrible man who tried to harm you, he yanked your head up, and that's when I recognised you.'

'How did you recognise me when you only saw me when I was a baby?'

TCG laughed, 'I remember the day when you told me you hate your dad, and he never visits you. Only if you knew that I used to fly to Britain to see you, which you had no knowledge of. I remember following you down the path once, and you were sitting in the field amongst the daisies. You were crying for your dad, and I just sadly watched you with an aching heart.'

Suddenly, Liana's voice sliced through the air like a blade. 'TCG, did you know I always wondered who my dad was?'

He glanced at her with a smirk tugging at the corners of his lips. 'TCG,' he repeated. 'Are you still going to call me by that name?'

Liana stared at him and rudely spoke. 'I will never call you dad if that's what you think!'

'I don't blame you...but why not?' TCG's question hung in the charged air.

'You don't deserve to be called dad,' Liana turned her face from TCG and started ignoring him. He tried to talk to her, but she didn't respond.

'You're so stubborn! Why can't you give me a chance to make things right between us?' he sighed. Suddenly, a loud noise reverberated throughout the house; TCG's instincts kicked in, and he sprang to his feet, fingers closing around the cold steel of his gun.

Adrenaline surged through his body as he moved towards the bedroom door. Every nerve in his body was on high alert.

He heard voices in the living room. 'Someone's broken in,' he urgently whispered to Liana, who looked startled and confused. 'Liana, quickly hide!' he commanded, urgency in his voice.

'I can't do this anymore,' she hissed.

'Look, there's no time, just hurry! Listen to me right now,' whispered TCG, trying his best to listen to the commotion downstairs. His earpiece suddenly started beeping, and he quickly answered.

'Is everything okay? Because our radar is detecting that danger has reached your location,' Officer Benjamin's voice came through the earpiece.

'Somebody has broken in,' whispered TCG.

'We're coming,' Benjamin assured him, and the line went dead.

TCG strolled out of the room and quickly looked around the hallway for any sign of danger. He peered over the bannister, but no one was there. The sound of people talking slowly disappeared. He slowly walked down the hallway towards the stairs, and then, the unmistakable click of a trigger being pulled sliced through the air. Instinctively, TCG ducked, and a bullet whizzed past him, missing him by inches; he spun around, and to his surprise, there stood a teenage girl.

She stood with pride and arrogance. Her black leather jacket looked like the midnight sky, and the silver zippers gleamed like hidden daggers, ready to be unsheathed. Her high heels, sleek and beautiful, elevated her figure. Her heels whispered promises of danger; she wore them like a badge of honour, a proclamation that she belonged to the evil shadows.

Mahogany hair cascaded over her shoulders. Strands caught the sunlight, turning them into threads of spun gold. Her sharp brown eyes bore witness to countless secrets and evilness. Her blood-red lips curved into a smile that dared the world to challenge her.

She pointed her gun straight towards TCG's chest. He, however, seemed as if he wasn't afraid at all. He laughed mockingly at her. 'Bad aiming, lass,' he taunted. 'You just missed me, you dumb cow.'

Her lips curved into a smirk. 'I intentionally missed to get your attention,' she retorted. 'I don't kill behind a person's back. I'm not a loser like you!'

'And I don't fight bitches,' TCG declared, his voice dripping with hatred. 'I only fight men. Do you understand?'

The girl's snigger cut through the air. 'Your downfall was because of your wife and daughter,' she teased. Her words were like a sharp knife stabbing into TCG's heart, but he kept it cool. 'And if you want to fight men,' she continued. 'You're more than welcome.'

Unexpectedly, a man appeared from behind the girl.

'Kevin Lee, ya bastard!' muttered TCG, tightening his grip on his gun. And then, without any warning, another man came running up the stairs and stood beside the girl. He was Fang's bodyguard, Edward.

Suddenly, firing could be heard from downstairs. TCG knew Steven and his crew had come, starting the inevitable war with anyone lurking downstairs.

TCG lunged at Edward, catching him off guard with an unexpected kick to the face. He spun around and shot Kevin, wounding him in the arm. Kevin retaliated by firing at TCG, who swiftly ducked the bullets. However, a bullet struck TCG in the arm, making him scream in anger.

He sprinted down the hallway as Kevin and Edward started running after him. Quickly glancing over his shoulder, he pointed his gun towards Kevin and fired. A bullet sliced through the air and tore through Kevin's side. As he fell to the ground, he shot a bullet at TCG.

TCG swore out of pain as he felt the bullet skim his forearm. He immediately stopped running and leaned against a wall for support; the pain was unbearable, causing him to grit his teeth. Edward took advantage of the situation and ran towards TCG to inflict more damage on him. But what he didn't know was that when TCG was inflicted with pain, it made him angrier. He swung a heavy fist in Edward's face, causing him to grab his face in agony.

The dimly lit hallway reverberated with the rhythmic thud of combat boots against the cold tiles. TCG moved with lethal grace, his body a coiled spring ready to strike. Opposite him stood Edward, his eyes narrowed in determination and revenge.

They were both masters of their craft, kickboxing and martial arts; the air crackled with tension as they circled each other. 'You're going to wish you were never born!' yelled TCG, glaring into Edward's eyes.

'You're going to wish you were still a toddler in your nappies!' smirked Edward.

TCG's movements were calculated and coordinated. His jet-black hair clung to his forehead, and his eyes gleamed with revenge. A scar ran down the side of his face, a testament to countless battles fought and won.

Edward, who was taller and broader, flexed his knuckles. TCG lunged, his foot aiming for Edward's chest. Edward deftly sidestepped, countering with a spinning back kick. TCG blocked it, his forearm absorbing the impact. He grinned and spat. 'Not bad, soldier,' he taunted. 'But I think you forgot who I am. I'm Triple Caste Gangster.'

Edward didn't respond. Instead, he continuously struck him with hooks, jabs, and kicks. TCG swayed, evading each blow with precision. He applied his kickboxing and martial arts talent on Edward; he was a man of true skill and violence. Edward's frustration grew; he had never faced such a tough opponent before.

TCG seized the moment. He swept Edward's legs, sending him crashing to the floor.

Edward swore, rolling away just in time to avoid TCG's heel smashing into his skull, but TCG was relentless; he pursued Edward, striking his body with fists and kicks like a violent storm.

Edward's vision blurred; his ribs screamed in protest, and he tasted blood in his mouth, which seeped from his busted lip. Desperation fuelled him, and he twisted onto his side, aiming a low kick at TCG's knee. TCG hopped aside, avoiding the furious strike. Edward suddenly stood up and lunged towards him, wrapping his arms around his waist from the front and slamming him against the wall. For a moment, TCG's eyes widened in surprise, and then he grinned, his teeth stained red with blood. 'You've got guts,' he rasped. 'But guts won't save you today!'

He drove his fist into Edward's stomach, forcing him to release TCG; Edward staggered, gasping for air. TCG spun, delivering a spinning hook kick that sent Edward sprawling onto the floor; he struggled to rise. TCG took his chance, pinning him to the ground with his knees on his back. Edward's mind raced; he couldn't lose the fight. With a loud roar, he summoned his last reserve of strength. His hand shot up, fingers aiming for TCG's eyes. TCG dodged, but unfortunately for him, Edward's thumb grazed his left eye.

TCG flinched, momentarily blinded; Edward seized the opportunity, flinging TCG off him and quickly standing up. TCG and Edward tackled each other. They crashed to the floor, grappling like feral animals. The hallway seemed to shrink, suffocating them both.

With strength and power, TCG stood up with Edward's arm around his neck. He dug his teeth into Edward's neck like a hungry wolf. Blood seeped from Edwards's flesh, and he let out an agonising scream with a mixture of pain and anger.

TCG, whose teeth were sharper than a prana's, dug deeper into Edward's flesh, causing deep cuts to appear on his neck. Edward's shriek echoed throughout the hallway as TCG released him. He put his hand on his neck and glanced at TCG, who was spitting blood and flesh out of his mouth.

But Edward wasn't a person who gave up that easily. He charged at him again and struck TCG in the chest with a front snap kick followed by a talented spinning back kick straight into his face. TCG stumbled backwards as another skilful kick struck his face.

TCG, who was flaming with anger, suddenly grabbed Edward's neck with both his hands and banged his face into his knee. Then he slammed his fist into his nose, causing him to fall to the ground. 'Normally, I just shoot and kill, but you know what? I'm going to make you go through some bad boy pain before you die!'

TCG grabbed his gun and banged it three times into Edwards's nose and once into his head; blood painted his face and stained his clothes. Edward tried to shoot back at TCG, but instead, TCG twisted Edward's hand, causing the gun's muzzle to press into Edward's shoulder.

'Pull the bloody trigger!' yelled TCG. He pressed Edward's finger against the trigger. A shot rang out, and a bullet pierced into his shoulder. 'Did your gun backfire on you? 'Cause I think it did,' sniggered TCG.

Edward screamed in agonising pain. 'Triple Caste Gangster, if you're going to kill me, do it now. I'm not scared, and yeah, my posse is going to kill you!'

'I'll see what the shitheads do!' laughed TCG. 'Now say your last prayer!' and as he said those scornful words, he shot him in the chest and head.

TCG quickly ran through the hallway and put another bullet into Kevin, who was on the floor trembling with the other bullet still lodged in his side. He ran into Liana's room, but she wasn't there.

He sprinted down the stairs, his heart pounding and sweat trickling down his face. At the bottom of the stairs, he found Steven and Benjamin both out of breath. Blood trickled down their arms, evidence of the struggle they'd just endured. 'Where's Liana?' shouted TCG, looking around quickly.

'Here she is!' a sudden voice cut through the tension; TCG spun around to see the teenage girl. She held her gun confidently in her hand, and behind her was Liana tied to a pillar. A fabric gag muffled her cries, and her eyes were wide with fear, shattering TCG's heart.

'Liana!' he shouted, running towards her. The teenage girl slyly watched him sprinting towards Liana and smirked.

Steven's eyes widened. He recognised the danger. The girl held a matchstick, its tip glowing. 'No, TCG!' Steven's warning came too late.

The girl quickly threw the matchstick. It flew through the air, landing on a trail of gunpowder which she had carefully laid in front of Liana.

Instantly, fire erupted, causing TCG to stumble backwards with shock and fear. Flames roared and aggressively jumped upwards, much higher than his height. Through the fiery haze, he could see Liana struggling to get free from the tight ropes that tied her to the pillar.

'TCG, we need to get out of here!' Steven's voice cut through the chaos.

'I can't!' TCG shouted back, desperation in his eyes. 'I'm not leaving my daughter behind!'

As the flames started to consume the grand mansion, Benjamin and the remaining crew members scrambled backwards, their faces etched with fear. The harsh scent of smoke hung heavy in the air, and the wailing fire alarms pierced their eardrums like desperate cries for help.

TCG fought against the heat and smoke, focusing on Liana, who was tied to the pillar. The fabric gag muffled her cries, but her eyes were wide and terrified, showing how scared she felt. She was his daughter, and he had to help her.

The flames increased, causing all the officers to lose sight of TCG and Liana. Steven and Joseph tried to look for TCG through the thick and huge flames. 'There!' Joseph cried, pointing towards the flames. 'I think that's him!' he shouted, coughing on his words. Steven was about to run towards TCG but failed to do so. A part of the ceiling collapsed, sending showers of sparks and embers everywhere. The fire started to spread, consuming everything in its path.

'We've got to get out of here!' Steven yelled, smoke clawing at his throat.

All the officers started running towards the front door, escaping into the cool air. Outside, their police cars were parked with their emergency lights flashing. Officers swarmed everywhere, arresting some of the men who broke into TCG's house and slapping handcuffs on them.

Sergeant Andrew's eyes scanned the dilemma. 'Where's TCG and Liana?'

Joseph, still coughing, sadly shook his head, 'They didn't make it out.'

Steven's heart raced. He could hear sirens and screams, 'I don't know if they'll make it out of there!' he shouted, eyes fixed on the blazing mansion. The firefighters were on their way, but would they arrive before it was too late?

Fire danced in front of Liana, separating TCG from her. 'Liana!' shouted TCG as he saw her struggling against the ropes. His gaze darted around, seeking a solution, and then he caught sight of a rug. He picked it up and hurled it onto the flames, creating a narrow path towards her.

He ran towards her. 'I'm here,' he assured Liana, untying the fabric gag. She gasped for air as he continued to undo the strong knots which tied her to the pillar.

The flames increased rapidly around them, scorching their skin and making every breath a struggle. 'One more knot, and you'll be free,' TCG coughed, determination in his eyes. Liana stumbled forward as he finally freed her. 'Run!' he shouted, pointing towards the kitchen, where the flames seemed less. Liana stumbled towards the kitchen, coughing and choking on the thick smoke.

TCG was about to run behind her, but his escape was cut short; pain exploded in his side, a bullet had struck him. He grabbed his side in agony. Blood seeped through his trembling fingers, dripping on the floor, his vision blurred, knees buckling. He had to help Liana, even if it meant sacrificing himself. But his legs gave way, and he collapsed.

A sudden hand yanked his head up, and there she stood, the girl who had ignited the fire, 'They call me Eulalia,' she taunted. TCG's limbs were weak and tired; he remained paralysed and helpless.

Liana turned around when she heard the sudden mocking laugh. 'TCG! Get up, now!' she yelled hysterically.

'My revenge will be a bloody lovely one,' smirked Eulalia, drawing a machete from her belt.

'Noooo!' Liana screamed, sprinting back towards TCG.

'You thought you could kill my dad and get away with it,' Eulalia sneered, 'You're a daft bastard.' Without hesitating, she drove the machete into TCG's side, slicing through his skin.

TCG gasped as if the very air was strangling him; his body gave up, and he remained flattened on the floor with blood pooling beneath him, 'No!' Liana cried, her world shattering into pieces as she sobbed hysterically. Raging with anger, she ran towards the girl. At the exact moment, Eulalia spun around to defend herself, but it was too late. Liana's powerful kick struck her viciously in the face, sending her flying backwards.

Liana, fuelled by adrenaline, struck with precision, her fist connecting squarely with Eulalia's cheek. The impact caused Eulalia to fly backwards, landing on her hands and letting go of the blood-stained machete.

Eulalia tried to stand up quickly. Her eyes were fixed on the machete, and she was choking on the thick smoke that enveloped her. But Liana seized her chance, snatching the machete from the floor. Eulalia stared at her with anger in her eyes, assessing the immediate threat. The room crackled with tension, and the machete gleamed brightly, its blade hungry for blood. Liana's heart pounded; she knew this was her opportunity to end Eulalia's life.

Eulalia's gaze held a mix of fury and desperation, like a wounded predator cornered by an angry prey.

'You dare try to stab me, bitch!' she bellowed, rage and hatred decorating her evil features.

Liana charged, machete clenched in her trembling hand. Talented and cunning, Eulalia quickly sidestepped and seized Liana's arm with her right hand, fingers digging deep into her flesh. She then gripped her left hand around Liana's throat, forcing her head backwards. The world blurred, and Liana's mind focused on killing Eulalia.

Liana pivoted, summoning every ounce of strength, and the machete found its mark, sinking into Eulalia's abdomen. A guttural gasp escaped her lips; she grabbed the weapon's hilt, 'No!' Eulalia gasped, with blood pooling around the blade. Liana's grip remained unyielding. Hatred and fury surged within her. With a scream, she pushed the machete deeper into Eulalia's flesh, causing her to shriek loudly, eyes wide with agony and fear.

Liana let go of the machete, and with all her remaining strength, she kicked Eulalia in the chest with a powerful front snap kick. Eulalia fell into the fire, flames angrily consuming her. Liana stood amidst the scorching flames, chest heaving; the taste of victory felt nice. The room cracked with fire, and the machete lay discarded on the floor, a silent witness to the brutal fight that had just occurred. Liana spun around towards TCG; he lay motionless, a fragile figure amidst the inferno.

'Dad, get up!' she cried, desperation clawing at her insides, but he remained unresponsive, lost in the smoky haze.

Flames erupted everywhere, their fiery tongues licking at the crumbling walls. Smoke had consumed the air, suffocating her. Huge flames surged towards her feet, their heat searing her skin. She gasped, her lungs craving for oxygen, yet each breath tasted of ash and despair.

The remaining section of the ceiling groaned, warning her of what was to come. Suddenly, TCG's hand stirred, a sign of life.

'Dad!' Liana's cry echoed through the chaos. His eyes remained shut. She seized his blood-stained arm. Energetically, she swung it behind her neck, 'Come on, stand up!' she cried. TCG unexpectedly gasped and shockingly stood up, holding onto her for his dear life, his movements slow and desperate. Blood dripped down him and stained her clothes in a terrifying bright red.

Liana stumbled forward, her legs shaking under his weight, but she pressed on, one foot in front of the other. Heading towards the kitchen, she spotted the door keys through tear-filled eyes on a nearby unit. She slowly lowered TCG on the floor. Her breaths were ragged as she snatched the keys with trembling fingers. Their cool metal felt like a lifeline. Liana stumbled towards the door, seeking refuge and salvation. Her trembling fingers fumbled with the lock. She heard a click, and the door swung open; a rush of fresh air hit her.

But life was never easy. The once sturdy kitchen unit on the left side of the door crumbled. It fell in front of the doorway. Liana's escape route vanished, replaced by a mountain of wood. She glanced back at TCG, sprawled on the floor, blood staining his clothes. Desperation clawed at her throat.

With a cough, she quickly picked up the broken pieces of the unit and threw them to the side. She needed to hurry; flames were racing towards the kitchen, consuming everything in its path. Gasping for air, she picked up more pieces of wood, flinging them out of the way.

TCG's weak form was blurred through her tears as she glanced towards him. Summoning a bit more strength, Liana picked up the last pieces of the broken wood, clearing the doorway.

She quickly reached for TCG, and together, they stumbled into the fresh air, the flames fading behind them.

Outside, chaos erupted. Benjamin quickly pointed towards the burning mansion, his voice urgent and astonished. 'There's TCG and Liana! Hurry, we need a medic ASAP!'

The paramedics and police officers sprinted towards them. As they ran towards them, Liana suddenly collapsed on the ground, dragging TCG down with her. She clung to him, their shared survival a fragile piece of thread.

Chapter Fifteen
Lost your memory! Remember me!

Liana's eyes slowly opened, and a beeping noise echoed in her ears. Light seeped through the window, and she slowly sat up. The room smelled of medicine, and the white walls seemed to close in on her.

A sudden soft voice broke the silence, 'You're awake,' said a nurse, her soothing smile putting Liana at ease. On her name tag was written 'Nurse Lilly.'

'Where am I?' Liana murmured, her gaze darting around the room. The bed creaked as she shifted, and her body protested with a dull ache.

'Sweety, you're in the hospital,' Nurse Lilly replied kindly. Her eyes held a mix of compassion and sorrow as if she'd seen countless patients like Liana before.

Everything slowly sank into Liana's confused mind. She had been brought to the hospital after escaping from the burning mansion. The memory of the fiery mansion was hazy, like a dream she couldn't quite grasp, but something more worrying concerned her. 'Where's my dad?' she whispered, her voice trembling.

Suddenly, another nurse stepped into the room. 'Nurse Molly' was written on her name tag. 'Liana, dear. Your dad is in the adult ward,' she said calmly. Her eyes held a hint of sympathy as if she understood Liana's trauma.

Liana glanced at Molly with pain in her eyes, 'Can I see him?'

'I'm sorry, dear,' Lilly said gently, her gloved hand resting on Liana's shoulder, 'you're too weak to move from this room. Your body needs all the rest it can get.'

'No, I want to see him now!' Liana's desperation surged. She felt like a captured girl, clinging to a false hope of reuniting with her father. Abruptly, the computer on the desk beside her bed started beeping loudly. The two nurses rushed to it, fiddling with the tubes connected to Liana's oxygen supply, and the room buzzed with urgency. Liana's heartbeat started to slow down, and her breathing became difficult.

'My dear,' smiled Lilly, her eyes crinkling at the corners. 'Your oxygen is running low. You need to rest. I'll be taking care of you.' Her voice held a promise, a lifeline in this unfamiliar place.

Liana glanced at Molly, hoping she would agree to take her to TCG. But Molly just shook her head, her fingers quickly flicking through a bunch of documents.

'Get Liana some food, Molly,' Lilly instructed. 'She'll feel much better if she eats.'

Molly put the documents on a desk and left the room. Liana sighed, sinking back against her pillow. She felt sick and weak; the hospital room felt both comforting and depressing, a place where life hung in a delicate balance.

As Lilly adjusted the oxygen tubes, Liana closed her eyes, hoping for strength and healing. She wondered if her dad was okay. Was he going to survive the brutal stab he got? The rhythmic beeping of the machines became her lullaby, and she drifted into a peaceful sleep, dreams and reality blending into one.

'Liana dear!'

Liana's eyes snapped open, and there stood Molly with a tray of food in her hands, 'Here, eat this. You'll feel better,' she said, smiling softly at Liana as she placed the food tray on her bed.

Liana nibbled at the food, her gaze shifting between Lilly and Molly. They moved around her bed, focusing on the computer screen and on a file of documents. 'You look much better,' Lilly said, suddenly turning to Liana with a reassuring smile. She removed the oxygen pipes from her.

'Can I see my dad now?' Liana whispered, a small smile tugging at her lips.

'No, you can't!' Lilly's voice suddenly seemed harsh, her eyes narrowing. 'You cannot leave this room. Are my words understood or not?' Her sternness cut through the air, making Liana erupt with anger.

She flung her blanket aside, determination fuelling her, 'No, your words are not understood!' she snapped, jumping off the hospital bed and sprinting towards the room door.

'Where do you think you're going?' Lilly's shout echoed as she grabbed Liana's arm. Liana struggled, desperate to break free from her grasp.

Molly stepped forward, her touch gentle as she wiped Liana's tears, 'It will be better for him and you if you just rest,' she whispered softly.

'I want to see if he's all right!' Liana sobbed.

'He's in good condition,' Molly assured her, her eyes locking onto Liana's, 'And he'll feel much better if he knows you're resting.'

Liana returned to her bed; her steps were heavy, and her heart felt tight. Annoyance and longing battled within her, but exhaustion suddenly overpowered her. She slowly laid down on the bed, and sleep claimed her again.

'She's in room number fourteen in the children's ward...and he's in room twenty-one in the adult's ward.'

Liana's senses stirred as she awakened from her slumber. The air tasted of antiseptic, and the hum of machinery made a disturbing noise.

Her eyes adjusted to the clinical surroundings: the white walls, the clean furniture, and the faint scent of antiseptic. Lilly stood at the room's far end, looking out from the vast window, her back facing Liana.

Liana wondered what lay outside. She could hear Lilly speaking calmly, 'I'm repeating it. She's in room number fourteen,' she murmured into her phone, 'And Triple Caste Gangster is in room number twenty-one, adults' ward.'

Liana's brow furrowed; why was Lilly discussing her and her Dad? And why was she using his gangster name in the hospital? The use of his gangster name sent a shiver down her spine.

Lilly spun around, her eyes widening as they met Liana's, 'You're awake,' she spoke in a shocked voice.

'Is there a problem?' Liana's voice was sharper than she intended it to be. She swung her legs over the edge of the bed, urgency propelling her towards the door, an escape route, a chance to find out where her dad was.

'You bloody annoying girl!' Lilly's tender tone vanished, replaced by a lion's roar. She sprinted after Liana, trying to wrench her hand away from the door handle, but Liana had gained her strength by now. She swiftly kicked Lilly in the shin, causing her to squint her eyes and stumble backwards in pain. Liana didn't hesitate and yanked the door open. She sprinted into the corridor, heart pounding, questions running in her mind. The hospital's corridors blurred as she sprinted, fuelled by adrenaline. She had to find her dad!

Liana's heartbeat increased as she darted through the corridors. The white walls blurred as she ran, and the scent of freshly mopped marble clung to her like a second skin. Her bare feet slapped against the linoleum floor, each step a desperate plea for answers. Room numbers flashed by, a countdown towards the truth. Nurses scurried past, their eyes flickering with curiosity, but Liana had no time for gossip. She was on a mission to find her father.

Nurses walked in and out of rooms. She could see other patients, a crying child, a doctor's hushed conversation with an older woman, and a sick boy vomiting. But Liana's focus remained on finding room twenty-one.

Suddenly, room twenty-one materialised before her. She hesitated, her hand trembling as she gripped the handle. Liana could hear Lilly's heavy footsteps getting closer. She felt nervous opening the door; what awaited her inside? Perhaps her weak father, or would it be someone else entirely?

Liana pushed the door open, the hinges protesting with a low creak. The room smelled of antiseptic and despair; her eyes instantly fell upon TCG, lying in a narrow bed, staring at the ceiling.

'Hi, Dad,' Liana whispered, her voice barely audible. She stepped closer, her heartache threatening to suffocate her. 'It's me, Liana.' TCG remained unresponsive, his gaze fixed on the ceiling tiles. The room seemed to hold its breath, and the air hung heavy with unspoken tensions.

Liana slowly walked towards him, whispering gently, 'Dad, I have come to see how you are!' But TCG's eyes remained distant. Devoid of emotion, he continued staring upwards as if lost in a world beyond anyone's reach.

'Dad!' Liana hissed, her grip tightening on his cold hand, 'We need to get out of here. I think your enemies are catching up to you!'

TCG yanked his hand out of hers, and his response was sharp, cutting through the silence like a blade: 'I don't know what you're talking about, you stupid little girl!' His voice held no warmth and comfort.

'Your enemies know you're here,' Liana insisted, her urgency increasing, 'We have to leave, RIGHT NOW!'

But TCG's expression remained blank and unyielding. 'Dad!' Liana shouted in panic, her heart pounding. She watched as he suddenly moved his face away from her. 'Why won't you listen to me?' she yelled.

And then, a soft voice suddenly spoke, 'I'm sorry, dear.' Liana spun around to find a woman doctor standing behind her. Her eyes were filled with pity and sympathy,

'What do you mean you're sorry?' Liana's tears welled up, threatening to spill over.

The doctor gazed into Liana's tearful eyes, 'Your father has lost his memory,' she explained gently, 'I've seen this happen to a lot of patients. I've been a doctor for twenty years, and most people that I've seen suffer from this illness have never regained their memory.'

Liana sank onto the edge of the bed, her world crumbling; she buried her face in her hands, tears flowing freely, her throat tightened with grief, and she wondered how many memories she'd now carry alone.

The weight of it all threatened to consume her. Her tears flowed like a river, trickling down her cheeks and onto her hands. Through the blur of her anguish, something bright caught her eyes.

She wiped away her tears with the back of her hand and caught sight of the delicate silver necklace that hung around her neck. The blue heart pendant held secrets that she wasn't aware of. Liana's trembling fingers brushed against the cold heart, and memories suddenly burst forth. Images of laughter, joyful smiles, and whispered promises flooded her senses.

TCG, the one who had destroyed his life to save her, was lying there, staring blankly at the ceiling. Once vibrant and full of life, his eyes seemed unhappy, tearing at Liana's soul.

She unclasped the necklace without hesitation and placed it in TCG's palm. His skin was cool, almost lifeless. 'Please remember me,' she whispered, her voice barely audible. The words carried the weight of a thousand shared moments, a plea to remember what had been lost.

TCG's gaze shifted downward. Confidence decorated his face, and his fingers closed around the pendant. For a fleeting moment, Liana saw a flicker of recognition, but then he looked up at her, all confused.

Liana's world was left empty now, tears streaming down her cheeks, mirroring the rain outside. It was as if the world was weeping with her.

He slowly touched the pendant, tracing its curves softly and gently. Was it a mere ornament to him now, or did he still remember the love that the necklace held?

Liana couldn't bear the uncertainty; she squeezed his hand, hoping he would remember the times they laughed together, the dangerous situations they fought off, and the secrets they had shared.

Suddenly, Liana felt herself getting yanked away from TCG. She looked up and saw Lilly looking down at her with an evil grin. She tightened her grip around Liana's arm and laughed aloud in her face.

A man, clad in black, unexpectedly barged into the room, causing the doctor to look at the man and then at Lilly, who was holding Liana. 'What are you two doing in here?' she asked.

'Just shut your trap before I shoot you!' smirked the man, glaring at the doctor. She quickly took a few steps back, fear overwhelming her.

He strolled towards TCG and smirked, 'I see you look confused!'

'Get away from my dad!' yelled Liana.

The doctor gasped and glanced at Liana, who was struggling to get free from Lilly's tight grip, 'It's going to be lovely shooting your daughter in front of you!' the man whispered and swiftly pulled his gun out from his pocket.

Liana let out a painful shriek and struggled to get free, but her struggles made Lilly tighten her grip around her arm with even more strength. TCG slowly looked down at the necklace and then at Liana. He squinted his eyes and then suddenly blurted out, 'Let go of my daughter, you bloody bitch!'

Chapter Sixteen
Dead together! Down forever!

The doctor's scream sliced through the charged air as she saw the man pointing the gun towards Liana. Panic surged within her, and she instinctively ran towards the door, but the angry and determined man blocked her path. His grip on the gun tightened, and he aimed it straight at her head, forcing her to retreat.

Lilly continued to stand stubbornly, still holding Liana by the arm. Liana's eyes darted between the evil man and the doctor.

His lips curled into a cruel smile as he turned his gun back towards Liana, 'Say goodbye to your daddy,' he taunted.

TCG glanced at the necklace. It was as if the blue pendant suddenly brought memories back one by one. The images of him and Liana sinking underwater appeared. He remembered how he cradled her and said, 'I will never leave you.' Black Hawk's lifeless body flashed before his eyes, Fang's sinister figure emerged, and the way the mansion erupted into flames. Amidst all these memories, he held onto the most loved memory, Liana's smile. He glanced at her, memories hitting him like a powerful tide. The image of Naila appeared before him; he remembered how he had gently held her hand and softly whispered in her ear, 'I promise, I'll keep our daughter safe.'

TCG shoved the necklace into his pocket and sprang into action. His eyes scanned the room, seeking any advantage. His gaze fell upon the metal food tray neatly placed on the nearby desk. He snatched it up without hesitation and flung it at the man's face. The tray hit him directly in the face with a loud clang, momentarily blinding the intruder.

In that split second, the man's finger tightened on the trigger, the gunshot reverberated, and TCG's instincts kicked in. He ducked, the bullet skimming his hair. Adrenaline surged through his veins as he sprinted towards the assailant.

The man recovered from the bang he got in the face. Fury decorated his features, and he fired again, but TCG executed a flawless dodge. Ducking and evading the deadly bullet with precision, he delivered a swift roundhouse kick into the man's face, causing blood to spray from his broken nose. The gun nearly slipped out of his grasp, but he fought to regain control of it. TCG seized the opportunity. He slammed the man's head against the wall, baffling him. Twisting the intruder's arm behind his back, TCG seized the gun. 'Where's William Archer, the ass wipe?' His voice was low and menacing

Lilly, desperate and cornered, pulled a gun out of her pocket. She aimed the gun straight at Liana's head. With an angry and evil face, she hissed, 'Triple Caste Gangster, if you shoot him, then I'll shoot your damn daughter.'

TCG looked back at his daughter and then shifted his gaze to Lilly, 'Go on,' he challenged. 'Let's see you try it!' he shouted. With one swift movement, he pointed the gun towards Lilly and fired. The gunshot echoed through the room, and Lilly fell to the floor, letting go of Liana.

The doctor rushed towards Liana, gently holding her arm, 'Come on,' the doctor urged, 'let's get out of here. It's dangerous.' They ran out of the room, leaving TCG to confront the man.

'I don't know where William Archer is,' said the man, his voice trembling.

'Really?' TCG sneered, 'You don't have a damn clue where your boss is?' He slammed the gun into the man's forehead, causing blood to trickle down his face.

'OK, OK,' the man blurted out, his voice trembling with panic. 'He's waiting for me in Rose Hill Carpark!'

'Thanks for the info, bro,' TCG laughed, his eyes narrowing, 'Have you got anything else to spit out, or are you done?'

The man quivered, his silence confirming his fear, 'I'll take that as a no,' TCG concluded, his tone dripping with menace.

'Please don't kill me, I beg you!' the man pleaded, his voice trembling. TCG thought about Rose Hill Carpark, its dimly lit corners hiding more than just shadows. Without any further hesitation, he aimed the gun at the man's head and shot him twice, ending his life.

The room fell silent, and the air was thick with the scent of blood. TCG glanced at the gun he was holding, knowing the real battle was beginning. The hunt for William Archer had begun, and nothing would stop him now.

TCG ran out of the room, adrenaline surging through his veins. He went past many hospital corridors, scanning left and right, desperate to find his daughter. Alarms wailed, their shrill cries echoing off the walls. A robotic voice suddenly started to speak through the hospital speakers, announcing that the entrance and exit doors were about to shut.

'No, not now,' TCG muttered, taking deep breaths. Suddenly, someone yanked his head backwards and continued to hold him in that position. TCG could see the assailant's hand from the side of his eye, pulling out a knife from his pocket.

With his right foot, TCG quickly kicked backwards straight into the man's groin. He screamed with pain, causing him to release his grip on TCG's hair. TCG turned around and sent a powerful kick in the man's chest, causing him to stumble backwards.

The man quickly regained his footing and charged towards him with his knife glinting in the light. TCG hurriedly sidestepped, and his combat training kicked in. A swift kick to the man's leg sent him stumbling backwards; TCG ran towards him and struck him in the face with a spinning back kick followed by a skilful flying knee strike.

The man's vision blurred, blood squirting from his lip. Quickly regaining his focus, he lunged at TCG's chest with his knife. With much talent and skill, TCG unexpectedly stepped aside and grabbed the man's arm.

'Bloody hell!' yelled TCG, giving an uppercut to the man's face, 'have you ever had a broken arm, ya daft bastard? Cause if you haven't, you might as well taste the beauty of it today!' He twisted the man's arm behind his back and dragged him down to the ground. The man groaned in agony as he felt his arm getting dislodged. TCG took his chance, wrenching the knife out of his grasp and firing two shots into the man's head and chest. He collapsed onto the floor, helpless and defeated. Chaos erupted and screams sliced through the air as people saw what had happened.

TCG's voice cut through the panic. 'Ladies and gentlemen, I'm from the NYSA, New York's Secret Agency. Stay calm. I'm here to protect you.' He didn't officially work for the NYSA, but Andrew would call him in when things got out of hand. He was a ruthless gangster notorious for his habit of pinning assholes to the ground. Everyone suddenly fell silent on hearing his words, but the sirens continued to pierce through the air.

In a desperate race against time, TCG sprinted down the escalators, Liana's name reverberating in his mind like a drill going through a wall. His eyes suddenly caught sight of the doctor who had run out of the room with Liana, 'Where's my daughter?' TCG shouted, running towards the doctor.

'I was running down the corridor with her when a man snatched her from me and sprinted out of the hospital with her.' She was crying and trembling with panic and fear.

TCG's mind raced. The only place she could be was in Rose Hill Carpark. A sudden, searing pain erupted in his side, and he remembered that Eulalia had stabbed him. He gritted his teeth, fingers pressing against the wound.

As he approached the end of the conveyor belt, his legs trembled, and he stumbled to the floor. His surroundings blurred, and the wound gnawed at him, threatening to destroy his mission of trying to find his daughter. TCG attempted to rise, but his body protested, surrendering to the cold, unforgiving tiles.

As he struggled to stand up, he suddenly remembered Liana's fierce battle with Eulalia and how she had helped him through the burning mansion with love and devotion. He remembered her comforting smile and her sweet voice. They had both gone through a lot of pain, and TCG was not going to let Liana go through any more. With a newfound strength, he unexpectedly hauled himself up.

He slowly limped towards the exit doors. Liana's face reappeared in his mind, the way she fought, the way she cared. She was more than a girl; she was his daughter, and he had to find her. TCG stumbled forward, driven by love and sheer willpower. The exit doors loomed ahead. He had to get to her quickly.

'Liana, where can you be?' he whispered to himself, looking rapidly around.

'I'm sorry. Are you looking for Liana? She's outside,' sneered a man from behind TCG. 'You better run and catch up to her before she gets shot,' he smirked.

The man's mocking voice reverberated in TCG's mind, his grip tightened on the cold metal of his gun, 'Who are you?' he demanded, his voice low and dangerous.

'Why should I tell you that?' spat the man, arrogance decorated his face.

'Fine,' TCG spat, his patience waning. Without any hesitation, he pulled the trigger, killing the man instantly. The gunshot echoed through the lobby, a stark reminder of TCG's violence.

TCG ran towards the exit doors. A security guard stepped in front of him, 'No one is allowed to exit the building,' the guard declared firmly.

'Shut up, I'm from the NYSA, you better let me exit this damn hospital!' shouted TCG.

'I have been told not to let anyone exit the hospital. Do you understand me or not?' he shouted back.

TCG pointed his gun towards him and smirked, 'You better let me go, now, or I'll shoot you dead! Ass wipe.'

The guard hesitated, torn between duty and survival. TCG pointed the gun directly at his forehead. The guard finally surrendered. 'OK, hurry up and get past,' he muttered, eyes darting nervously around the lobby.

TCG ran outside into the fresh air. The morning breeze blew through his hair, and the sun shone in his eyes. He was about to press his earpiece to call for some backup, but he realised they were missing. 'Dumb doctors,' he muttered. 'They probably took it.' His frustration increased as he realised his phone was missing as well. 'Where's my bloody phone!' he yelled to himself.

TCG ran towards Rose Hill Carpark, desperation urging him forward. Suddenly, a familiar person stepped before him, and he instantly stopped running. 'Hey, TCG. Why in the world are you running like a cheetah? I thought you were meant to be in hospital!'

'Steven!' TCG gasped, his breath ragged. 'Hurry, call for backup! That bloody Fang, he's got my daughter! The shithead.' His voice cracked with fear as he yelled, adrenaline propelling him forward.

Steven sprinted after TCG, fingers flying over the buttons of his earpiece. 'Andrew, we need backup right now,' he urgently relayed.

They reached the dimly lit carpark, shadows dancing across the asphalt. TCG glanced back at Steven, his eyes wide. 'Don't let anyone see you,' he whispered, the weight of his gun a constant reminder of the stakes.

Steven slowly pulled a handgun out of his thigh holster, his green eyes scanning the carpark rapidly. 'Hey, no one's here,' he murmured.

Before TCG could respond, a voice blurted out, 'Hey, loser, are you looking for us?' TCG and Steven spun around, their eyes landing on

Fang and his menacing gang. Fang clicked his fingers and delivered a chilling command, 'Blood Beauty, bring the girl forward.'

Blood Beauty materialised from the murky shadows. Her fingers gripping Liana's trembling arms. TCG instantly locked eyes with Liana. Tears streamed down her cheeks; she just wanted this trauma to be over.

Before TCG could react, a gunshot reverberated through the carpark. A bullet tore through the air and struck him in the leg; it was a searing pain that caused his knees to buckle. He instantly collapsed onto the cold ground, his breath stolen by agony.

Blood squirted from the wound like a crimson fountain. It pooled beneath him, staining the earth, a testament to the violence that had just occurred.

'Dad!' Liana's desperate cry pierced the air. She tried to break free from Blood Beauty's tight grasp but failed to do so.

Steven quickly looked down at TCG. 'Are you alright?' he gasped. Without any hesitation, he suddenly started angrily shooting at Fang's men. The men didn't hesitate and started shooting back. Steven skilfully ducked behind a car, then quickly took his chance and started shooting again. His bullets tore through the air, hitting two men and killing them instantly.

A man, clad in black, slowly stepped out of the shadows, calmly aiming his gun towards Steven. He pulled the trigger, and a bullet pierced the air, hitting Steven in the side. He fell onto the ground, blood staining his police uniform.

Fang yanked Liana towards himself, fingers encircling her arm tightly. He whispered in her ear, a whisper that carried a promise of danger. 'You're about to witness your father's demise,' he murmured. His voice was like a sharp knife stabbing her heart. Each syllable sent shivers down Liana's spine.

TCG painfully lifted his head. With trembling fingers, he aimed his gun at one of the men and shot him straight in the chest. The man let out an agonising shriek and fell to the ground.

Fang's anger flared. 'Show Zak Ezra what he truly deserves!' he shouted, making Liana cry in panic and fear.

The man clad in black shot TCG again; the shot rang out, hitting TCG in the arm. His gun slipped from his grasp as he collapsed face forward, pain running through his wounded arm.

Fang laughed and flung Liana onto the floor. The cold floor pressed against her cheek, and the metallic tang of fear spread throughout her body. She had never felt so powerless and so utterly vulnerable.

TCG knelt on the cold floor, battered and defeated. His once proud attitude had shattered into pieces, replaced by fear and grief.

Fang's predatory footsteps were graceful as he strode towards his prey. He snatched TCG's gun from the floor, its metal cool against his palm.

Fang's voice was low and evil. 'You thought you could always interfere in my evil plans. Ya pisshead.' he hissed, 'but today, I'll show you just how wrong you were.' Liana, her eyes wide with terror, tried to rise, but Fang's scary gaze made her freeze in her spot. He raised the gun, aiming it at TCG's back. Liana's scream tore through the air, desperate and scared. The gunshot reverberated, hitting TCG in the back. His body jerked, and he let out an agonising shriek. Pain spread all over his body as blood seeped from the wound. Fang leaned down towards TCG, close enough to smell the heavy scent of blood, 'My true dream,' he whispered into TCG's ear, 'killing you in front of your daughter. Ya bastard'

He slammed the gun into TCG's face, splitting his lip. Blood seeped from the split, staining the floor. Fang's rage surged, 'You thought you were invincible, didn't you?' he taunted, 'But now you're not invincible anymore. You're a loser and a freak.' With a swift motion, he bashed the gun against TCG's neck, causing him to let out another painful shriek. He started to choke on his spit, and then suddenly, he spat out a mouthful of blood.

The world seemed to shrink; shadows closed in as Fang tightened his grip on TCG's hair; the man who had struck fear in his enemy's hearts now lay on the floor, bloodied, battered and defeated. Fang's eyes bore into TCG's, a predator scrutinising the final moments of his prey. 'And after I kill you,' Fang's voice was a vicious whisper. 'You know exactly what I'm going to do to your daughter. Don't you?' his words hung in the air, a promise of horrors yet to unfold. He stood up and kicked TCG in the face; blood squirted out of his nose, and his vision blurred. Fang let out a sharp laugh, pointing the gun towards TCG's head and resting his finger on the trigger.

Liana quickly stood up and sprinted towards Fang, her heart pounding. She lunged for the gun, but Fang was quicker. He slammed it against her cheek. 'Back off, girl,' he sneered, 'or you'll go down with your dad.'

TCG, bloodied and gasping for air, slowly turned his face towards Liana. He spat another mouthful of blood out, and his eyes met hers. 'We go down, we go down together,' he whispered.

Those words ignited a fire within Liana's heart. Her anger surged, and she struck Fang in the side with a swift kick, followed by an uppercut that sent him reeling.

He regained his focus and swung a punch at her, but she deftly dodged it, seizing his arm. 'You bloody jerk,' she spat. 'It's about time I put you into your grave!' She painfully twisted his arm behind his back and snatched the gun out of his hand.

Liana aimed the gun towards Fang and fired, hitting him in the side.

Suddenly, sirens wailed, and police cars screeched into the car park. Officers jumped out of their vehicles and started tackling the rest of the men, slapping handcuffs on their hands and shoving them in police vans.

But Fang wasn't done. He quickly regained his focus, desperation showing on his face. Blood dripped down his side, colouring his white clothes in bright red.

He pulled out a glimmering knife from his pocket. 'Your attitude is going to end today!' he shouted at Liana. 'I wanted to treat you nicely, but you have left me no choice but to kill you.' He viciously slapped her in the face, sending her flying onto the floor. The gun instantly fell out of her hand, skidding across the ground. He crouched down next to her and was just about to stab her in the heart when he heard a voice slice through the tension. 'Turn your bloody face this way, you shithead!'

Fang spun around, and in that split second, TCG unexpectedly grabbed the gun that had slipped out of Liana's hand and shot Fang twice in the shoulder and once in the abdomen, sending him crashing to the ground. He lay motionless, blood gathering around him.

Liana's world spun in chaos. The air tasted of blood, making her shiver. She quickly got up and sprinted towards TCG, her hand grabbing his hand as if it were her lifeline.

His once vibrant, glossy eyes now held a haunting emptiness; his face was so battered and bloodied that Liana felt as if she couldn't recognise him. TCG stared into Liana's blue eyes, and then he collapsed, falling backwards onto the unforgiving hard ground. Blood dripped out of his mouth, staining the floor with blood.

As Liana watched TCG sprawled on the floor, she heard a gunshot piercing the air. Pain exploded in her arm as a bullet found its mark, tearing through her arm and causing her to scream a heart-shattering cry.

Blood dripped from her wounded arm, staining TCG's hand, which she held tightly. Liana intertwined her bloody fingers with TCG's.

'Dad!' she gasped, tears dripping down her face. The word, dad, brought back memories. She remembered how he smiled at her, laughed with her and fought to protect her. 'I swear I love you with all my heart!' Her voice hung in the air, a fragile promise as TCG's eyes slowly closed.

The agonising pain in her arm was unbearable, causing her to flop her head onto TCG's bleeding arm. The world started to blur, and her senses began to fade, one by one; first, her hearing, the distant wail of sirens, and the frantic voices of police officers were all muffled. A feeling of drowning overcame her. Then her vision blurred; the lights of the police cars seemed like dancing distant stars. She blinked, trying not to blank out, but darkness started to creep in from the edges of her vision.

She clung to his hand with love and care in this crucial moment. Their lives were tangled together, woven into a complicated embroidery of pain and love.

And as the world slipped away, she held on, fingers intertwined, a silent promise that even when danger would come to them, they would face it together.

In that horrifying moment, Liana slightly lifted her head, looking at TCG's battle-worn face, blood trickling from his lip, nose and forehead. His eyes were flickering with pain and agony.

Liana's breaths came in shallow gasps, each one a desperate plea for fresh air, and then she whispered her final word. The word that held a lifetime of memories. 'Dad,' she gasped. It was more than a name; it meant everything to her. She poured all her love, longing, and unspoken secrets into that single word.

It was as if the soft word 'Dad' infused TCG with his last surge of strength. His grip tightened around her hand, fingers slipping through hers. She felt his heartbeat slow down and heard his breathing lessen. Their lives were woven together, threads of joy and sorrow, and now, she clung to him, the man who had sacrificed his life for her, wiped away her tears and whispered her name with happiness and care.

'Steven, TCG, Liana!' shouted Officer Kate, running towards them with panic and fear. Officer Joseph reacted swiftly, firing at the man who had just shot Liana in the arm, ending his life instantly. Kate's voice trembled as she screamed, tears trickling down her cheeks. The urgency of the situation hung heavily in the air, 'Quickly, call the ambulance right now!' she yelled.

Chapter Seventeen
Eight months later! Got a girl that's a fighter!

'I never knew you were such a skilled motorbike rider!' TCG exclaimed, his laughter dancing in the salty breeze. He held Liana's shoulders as he sat behind her on the motorbike, his eyes shining joyfully. 'You're riding it pretty fast, faster than the way I ride a motorbike,' he smiled as the wind blew through his black hair, sending it flying all over his face.

'Dad! What do you expect?' Liana's laughter enhanced in the warm air, 'I'm your daughter!' She suddenly parked her Kawasaki next to another slick motorbike. It was TCG's.

With a mischievous grin, TCG jumped off Liana's motorbike and onto his own. 'Race you to the seashore!' he challenged. They both revved their engines, the thrill of the competition painting their faces with delight and happiness.

As they reached the seashore, they jumped off their motorbikes and ran towards the water hand in hand. They sat down and started enjoying the lovely scenery. Liana sank her hands into the warm sand. Her gaze was fixed on the sparkling blue sea; TCG proudly watched her, his eyes dazzling with happiness. 'Your eyes,' he whispered, 'They're as blue as the ocean, just like your mother's.'

His phone interrupted their laughter, and he answered it with a playful smile, 'Hi Steven, what's up?' he greeted.

'Would you like to come to The Secret Organisation of New York and chill with us!' asked Steven.

'Sure, bro! I think Liana would love to come as well. She's Liana TGG,' he laughed, looking at her. Liana glanced at him with a huge grin across her face.

'What does TGG mean, I wonder?' laughed Steven.

'It means The Gangster Girl,' said TCG, smiling.

'That's cool, Ezra TCG and Liana TGG, both father and daughter, defo make a great team!' Steven's friendly laughter burst forth. 'Anyway, see you there, bye!'

'Sure, bro,' TCG replied, putting the phone down.

Liana's smile softened, and she leaned over towards her dad, 'Hey, Dad, I want to ask you something.'

'Sure, ask me whatever you want,' he cheerfully said.

Her eyes sparkled with curiosity, 'Why do they call you Triple Caste Gangster?'

TCG's smile held a hint of mystery. 'I've been waiting for you to ask that question,' he said. 'My parents despised evil, but their families loved evilness and committed unspeakable crimes. They killed innocents, stole, and waged war against goodness. When I was thirteen, my parent's family members caught up with them and killed them.'

'They killed your parents?' Liana gasped.

'Yes, sweetheart,' TCG replied, his voice breaking, 'I was sent to an orphanage, a place that I hated from my heart. There, I kept to myself, a silent observer. There were loads of children in the orphanage. Hundreds of languages echoed throughout the corridors, and I mastered them all. I became an expert in different cultures and traditions. That's why they call me Triple Caste,' TCG paused momentarily, 'And I always stuck to the shadows. That's why they call me Gangster!'

He leaned towards Liana, eyes gleaming, 'And if you look into my life, you'll understand that I'm definitely a gangster. What do you think?' he asked playfully.

'Dad, you're definitely a gangster,' Liana replied, her smile unwavering.

'And so are you,' TCG laughed, 'Once I've made someone an enemy, they stay as an enemy. That means I'll hunt them down no matter where they are. It's my motto, and it should be yours, too!'

'Sure, Dad,' Liana chuckled, 'I like the sound of that.'

'And a while ago, you said that my smile holds secrets,' Liana continued, 'what did you mean by that?'

TCG held her hand, and they gazed into the sea. 'Look at your reflection and then mine,' he said softly. Liana looked at their reflection, studying her features and then TCG's.

'We don't look alike,' she scrutinised, her eyes dancing with playful curiosity, 'My hair's blonde, and yours is as dark as midnight. My eyes are blue, and yours are black like a moonless night.'

'Yeah, but look at your smile and then at mine,' TCG smiled, 'Our smiles are identical!'

'Yep, you're right, Dad!' Liana declared, squeezing his hand. 'We've definitely got the same smile,' her voice sparkled excitedly. His strong and steady hand tightened around hers, and their fingers intertwined like the threads of a cherished memory.

The sun painted the sky in shades of turquoise and gold, casting a warm embrace upon the gentle waves that lapped at their feet. The blue sea stretched out, an endless expanse of tranquillity and peace.

Seagulls swarmed overhead, their calls a sound of joy. The sand beneath them was soft and warm, a perfect cushion for their bare toes. Liana's laughter bubbled forth, a melody that danced with the rhythm of the waves. She leaned into her father's shoulder, feeling safe and protected.

'And we've definitely got the same attitude,' TCG added, a grin spreading across his face.

'Sure, I know that, Dad!' Liana laughed, a melody of pure delight. She suddenly stood up and started sprinting, her bare feet imprinting the sun-kissed sand, leaving a trail of joy behind. 'Catch me if you can!'

Fuelled by laughter, TCG chased her, his heart racing with excitement. The sun, a golden witness, painted Liana's long blonde hair, each strand catching the light like spun gold.

As they ran alongside the sea, the waves played tag with their toes, a playful movement of foam and sand. The breeze whispered secrets to Liana, lifting her hair and sending it all over her face. Breathless but determined, TCG caught up to her, his hand grasping her shoulder. They collapsed onto the warm sand, the sun dipping towards the horizon. Liana's eyes held mysteries, and her smile enlightened the sky. 'My smile holds secrets,' she whispered. The soft wind carried her voice across the vast sea and bright sky.

TCG dipped his hand into his pocket. 'Here,' he smiled, pulling out the blue pendant necklace. He placed it gently around her neck and laughed, 'Always keep this necklace with you. It brought my memory back.'

'I will always wear it, just like my mother used to,' Liana whispered.

TCG hugged her, a smile spreading across his face. Together, they watched the sun melt into the water.

Suddenly, TCG's earpiece beeped; he pressed the button and answered, 'What's up, Joseph?'

'My radar is detecting some danger near Prince Road; we need you there, RIGHT NOW!' Joseph's urgent voice crackled through the earpiece.

'Sure, bro,' TCG replied, adrenaline surging through his veins. He loaded his mag, the metal clicks echoing in the air. Liana, ever determined, grabbed his arm, her eyes fierce with determination.

'Dad, I'm coming with you,' she declared.

TCG studied her face. Pride and affection decorated his features. 'Sure, you're The Gangster Girl,' he said, a hint of amusement in his eyes, 'Got your gun?'

'Yes, Dad,' she smiled, her grip on the weapon unyielding.

TCG's grin widened. Their hands intertwined, like those of a father and daughter, ready to face danger side by side. TCG locked eyes with her and laughed, *'WE GO DOWN, WE GO DOWN TOGETHER!'*

The deep meanings behind this story

Life can indeed be challenging, filled with moments of sorrow and grief. People may leave this world, and some may distance themselves from you for various reasons. Yet, amidst all this, remember that there will always be someone who loves you deeply, someone who would sacrifice everything for your happiness.

When someone goes to great lengths to protect you and keep you safe, it's important to appreciate their efforts and remain calm in every situation. Never be rude or bad-mannered, for you may not know the deeper reasons behind their actions. Sometimes, the most significant revelations come from understanding these sacrifices.

Take Liana, for instance. The most beautiful moment in her life was discovering that the person who had been protecting her with all his heart was her father. This realisation filled her with immense joy and gratitude, knowing that his love and dedication were boundless, a treasure to be cherished forever.

Cherish those who care for you, for their love is a precious gift that can bring light and happiness to your life.

Remember, plotting against others to harm, disgrace, or ruin their lives will ultimately lead to your own downfall. Instead, choose the path of integrity and kindness, for justice will always prevail. Let this choice guide you, inspiring you to do what's right.

Take Zak Ezra, for instance. He endured unimaginable pain, yet he never gave up. The most sinister of enemies sought to destroy him, but he stood firm, taking them down one by one. Despite the bullets and wounds, he pushed forward, illuminating the darkness with his unwavering courage and determination.

Let Zak's story inspire you to be brave and confident. Stand tall against adversity, knowing that your strength and resilience can light up even the darkest of times.

Always cherish the memories of those who have left this world. Their most incredible gift to you is their love and care, which will forever remain in your heart. Even if you don't have a physical keepsake to hold, remember that their love is the most precious gift of all. Let this thought brighten your heart and bring you comfort.

Take Liana, for example. Her father gave her a necklace as a reminder of her mother's love. But it wasn't the necklace that brought Liana joy; it was the memories behind it. She remembered how her mother lovingly cared for her as a baby, and those memories filled her heart with warmth and happiness.

Focus on the love and care they gave you, and let those memories bring light to your life.

The greatest treasure in life is the unwavering love of your Father.

Coming soon!

Chapter One
She's excited and has an attitude!
You're on fire, chill dude!

'What have you been up to lately, sweetheart?' TCG smiled, sinking into the sofa next to Liana. His hand rested on her shoulder, possessive and familiar.

'I've been chilling!' Liana laughed sharply, but her eyes remained glued to her phone. She swiped through messages and notifications, seemingly oblivious to TCG's presence.

'How's your new job going?' TCG leaned back and took his shades off like a cool dude. His gaze remained fixed on Liana, assessing her response.

'Brilliant!' Liana's enthusiasm was genuine, but her attention remained glued to the digital world in her palm.

'You still thinking 'bout takin' courses at NYSA?' TCG's voice held a hint of arrogance as if he knew her answer.

'Most likely not,' Liana sighed, her tone mixed with irritation and annoyance.

'Why not, Sweetheart? It's the best place to go where you can become just like me!' TCG sat up straight, his gaze fixed on Liana, who remained engrossed in her phone.

'Listen to me,' Liana's voice was sharp, her frustration evident. 'That's got nothing to do with you, whether I continue to take courses or not. And stop calling me 'Sweetheart'. I'm not a baby!' She leaned on the arm of the sofa, her gaze fixed downwards.

TCG abruptly stood up, towering over Liana; his laughter was mocking, 'It has everything to do with me,' he retorted, 'And I'll call you whatever the heck I feel like!' He glanced at her, annoyance etching his features, 'And bloody cut the crap! You've been glued to that damn phone since I stepped foot in your flipping house, not a single glance my way; what's your deal?'

'Whatever!' Liana muttered, rolling her eyes.

TCG lost his patience, 'What did you just bloody spit out?' His voice rose, demanding an answer. Liana remained silent, her attention still on her phone. TCG's finger slid under her chin, and he tilted her face upwards, 'Look at me,' he insisted, 'what did you just say?'

Liana's eyes narrowed, 'I said whatever!' she yelled, 'Now flipping leave me alone, you moron!' she turned her face towards her phone again, determined to ignore him.

A young man unexpectedly entered the room, causing a sudden distraction. 'What's up, Liss?' he asked, glancing at TCG quickly and then back at Liana.

'Tell this flipping guy to get away from me!' Liana snapped.

The young man's eyes darted towards TCG, 'Oh, I see!' he grinned.

TCG sat on the opposite sofa, studying him. 'Where have you been, Jaydon?' he inquired, a smirk spreading across his face.

Jaydon flicked his black fringe out of his eyes. 'Hanging out with my mates. Anyway, Liss, how did your exam go?' he laughed, brushing TCG off and sitting beside Liana.

Liana put her phone down and smiled at Jaydon. 'You won't believe it. I passed, and they said I was among the most intelligent students so far!'

TCG's eyebrows shot up, 'Wait, what? Have you already aced that test? You never told me!' His surprise was genuine.

'Liss, your hard work was defo a success then, wasn't it?' Jaydon grinned, deliberately ignoring TCG's astonishment.

Liana leaned towards Jaydon, her smile widening. 'Actually,' she said, 'all the hard work and effort you put in was the real reason I passed.'

Jaydon's hands gently rested on Liana's shoulders, pulling her closer. He leaned towards her, whispering something in her ear.

TCG's patience waned, and he glared at Jaydon, trying to catch the whispered words. But they remained elusive, lost in the air. Suddenly, Liana burst into laughter. She glanced at TCG with a mischievous look before returning to her hushed conversation with Jaydon.

TCG pulled his phone from his pocket, seeking refuge in local news updates. The headlines blurred as he scrolled, and his anger increased.

'Jaydon,' Liana's voice carried excitement, 'I want to show you something. You're going to like it,' she smiled, standing up and walking into the hallway.

Jaydon quickly sprang up from the sofa as TCG glared at him disgustingly. He locked his grey eyes into TCG's jet-black eyes and spoke cheekily. 'Chill, dude! Just because she's excited about me doesn't mean you have to burn with anger!' he exclaimed, slamming the living room door behind him.

'Cheeky idiot,' TCG muttered, returning his attention to his phone. He flicked through several phone numbers until he found Steven's and dialled it, 'Hi, Steve bro.'

'Hi, TCG, what's up?' asked Steven.

'Nothing really, I just thought I'd give you a bell.'

'Well, you sound banged out,' laughed Steven.

TCG sighed, stretching his arm behind his head, 'Just the usual crap with Liana,' he confessed, staring up at the ceiling. 'She is all over Jaydon, the shithead!'

'Take a chill pill, mate, that's life for you!' laughed Steven.

'I can't take a bloody chill pill. If Jaydon, the dumb shit, doesn't stay out of my way, I'm going to bang him out!' said TCG, getting up and walking off to the kitchen.

'Trusting you, you will definitely bang him out,' laughed Steven.

'I'm not joking. I really want to bash him up,' TCG retorted 'he's getting on my nerves, and more than anyone, Liana is pissing me off.'

'I know she's pissing you off,' sighed Steven, 'but I think you're taking your anger too far. Take it easy on her,' he advised.

'Take it easy! Did you just bloody say that?' yelled TCG, gulping down some Coke, 'You're out of your head!' his gaze shifted beyond the glass doors into the vast backyard, where the green expanse of the garden seemed to mock his inner trauma.

'She can sometimes be a pain, but she's also adorable,' chuckled Steven.

'I thought she'd ditch the teenage drama by now, but nope!' sighed TCG.

'She's nineteen; probably when she turns twenty, she won't be so arrogant,' Steven chuckled, as if age held the key to fixing Liana's attitude.

'Whatever,' TCG's frustration flowed through his veins. 'As she gets older, her attitude keeps piling up. Anyway, I've got to go, bro,' he muttered.

'Bye. See you sometime soon, and when I do, I hope it's not because you've broken Jaydon's head,' laughed Steven, his voice echoing through the phone.

'You bet,' laughed back TCG, putting the phone down. He walked through the hallway and heard Liana laughing from one of the rooms. She could fill the atmosphere with warmth, even when she wasn't visible.

Liana unexpectedly stepped out from one of the rooms with a smile across her face, her eyes sparkling like distant stars. TCG's heart raced. He'd always been drawn to her smile and the way her eyes sparkled with excitement. Without thinking, he grabbed her arm, his touch gentle yet firm.

'Liana, I'm going,' he whispered, his voice as soft as a summer's breeze. She looked up at him, her expression mixed with curiosity and annoyance.

'And yeah, is there anything you want from me?' said Liana in a cocky voice.

'You're coming with me,' he whispered, looking into her stubborn eyes. Jaydon walked into the hallway with a grin spread across his face, but it faded as he noticed TCG's firm grip on Liana's arm.

'Jaydon,' Liana addressed him. 'I'm going to go out for a bit.' Her tone was weary, as if she was afraid of something. Jaydon slowly nodded, his smile returning.

'OK, Liss,' he paused, and then, with a mischievous grin, he said, 'but make sure you're back before eight.' With that, he strolled into the living room, leaving TCG and Liana alone in the hallway.

Liana stepped out into the sun-drenched driveway, her eyes tracing the sleek lines of the Lamborghini parked there. The car's vibrant white paint seemed to shimmer in the light, a sign of power and speed. TCG leapt into the driver's seat and patiently waited for Liana to join him.

'So why did you want me to come?' Liana's voice dripped with frustration as she arrogantly slumped into the passenger seat.

'Why is it a damn burden on your shoulders if you come with me?' TCG's smirk was annoying as he accelerated onto the main road.

'TCG, what's your problem?' Liana's patience was wearing thin.

'My problem? I don't have any problem, but I can damn well see that you've got one!' he said in a loud voice.

'Just shut it!' Liana muttered under her breath.

'You know you...' TCG suddenly slammed his foot on the brakes. 'Have you got eyes? You blind git!' he leaned out of the window, shouting angrily at a man who had just pulled out in front of him from a side street.

The man lowered his car window and yelled, 'Calm down, you shithead! If you're having a bad day, don't take it out on me!' He revved his engine and sped away.

'Bloody shut your gob!' shouted TCG, accelerating to catch up with the man. He overtook the man and swore at him so rudely, leaving him gob-smacked.

'I bloody hate these flippin' road users! Anyway, what was I sayin' to ya?' he sighed, glancing at Liana. She stared out of the window silently, 'Listen,' TCG's tone softened, 'If I've done something to you that you don't like, tell me.'

Liana turned towards him, her eyes flashing with attitude and arrogance, 'You've done a lot of terrible things, you piece of shit!'

TCG parked over in a parking bay and turned the car off. 'I don't know what you're talking about,' he said, acting innocent.

'TCG, you damn well know exactly what you've done to me!' yelled Liana giving him dirty looks.

'Tell me about it, I'll fix it,' TCG offered with a cheeky grin.

'You can't bloody fix the past, TCG!' Liana shouted with tears in her eyes.

'Stop calling me TCG! Do you understand me?' he yelled, no longer tolerating her attitude.

'I can call you whatever the hell I want! And yeah, what do you want me to call you?' Liana's defiance flared, her anger matching his.

'Call me dad. You dumb cow!' TCG's anger burnt inside his heart like wildfire.

'Yeah, I've seen what type of dad you are,' Liana spat, 'Dads don't do the type of stuff you've done,' she screamed, wrenching the car door open. She was about to leap out when TCG's hand closed around her wrist.

'Where do you think you're bloody going?' he shouted, yanking her back in the car.

'Let go of me, you jerk!' Liana shrieked, wrenching her hand free. She jumped out hurriedly, slamming the door shut behind her and running as fast as possible. TCG leapt out of the car, pursuing her with determined strides.

'Liana, get back here!' he angrily yelled, a heavy plea that resonated through the wind; each syllable carried the weight of forgotten promises and unspoken regrets.

Liana didn't look back at him and ran at the speed of the wind; the world seemed to tilt as if trying to tell her to stop running.

The wind swirled and twirled around her, blowing through her long blonde hair, causing every strand to look like a hot flame.

She quickly glanced over her shoulder, her heart pounding, and there he was, TCG, persistent in his chase. His strides were purposeful, each step closing the gap between them. The fury in his eyes looked like a brutal storm.

Her breathing quickened, and anger struck her heart as he firmly gripped her forearm. She could feel the heat radiating from his fingertips, burning her skin with an intense eagerness that sent shivers down her spine. He forcefully turned her around and locked his piercing eyes in her ocean-blue eyes, which were burning with anger and unspoken longing.

The rest of the world seemed to fade away in that heated moment, leaving only the intensity of their locked gazes.

TCG sighed and, with a gentle touch, placed both his hands on her shoulders. The world seemed to hold its breath as if waiting for his next words. Then, in a voice that carried both urgency and concern, he shouted, 'Ya need to stop bloody listening to Jaydon, the arrogant son of a bitch!'

Also by Joseph Jethro:

- *Undercover Gangster: Blood Ties In The Shadows*
- *Secret Gangster: My Life is All About Violence*

Be sure to keep an eye out for Joseph Jethro's upcoming books:

- *Never Underestimate Girls: Will she unlock the truth or...?*
- *Osmond Jay*
- *Coiled Within!*
- *Life's twisted: Love's harsh.*
- *Ego Downfall*
- *Dangerous Street Boys!*
- *Nathanial Caspian: Hit Me Harder!*
- *Unzipped: The Same Ride!*
- *Beyond Prison Bars*
- *Triple Caste Gangster 3: Promise Me*
- *Life of Five: Where is it safe?*
- *DID: He's Hunting Himself*
- *Emric Ladislas: I Tried*

Don't miss out!

Visit the website below and you can sign up to receive emails whenever Joseph Jethro publishes a new book. There's no charge and no obligation.

https://books2read.com/r/B-A-TDFLC-NRGCF

BOOKS 2 READ

Connecting independent readers to independent writers.

Milton Keynes UK
Ingram Content Group UK Ltd.
UKHW031201241024
450188UK00004B/315